I0547505

The Reluctant Conformist

Richard H Cowley

Published by Triskelion House 2020

Published: Triskelion House

2nd Edition

ISBN:978-1-910006-08-5

DEDICATION

To Magnus's forebears and descendants:
Both identified and not so.

APPRECIATIONS AND THANKS

This novel would have remained a sheaf of papers on a dusty shelf without the patience and encouragement of David Seth Iball, the Triskelion House fixer and publisher. This man's dedication to broadening the scope of new and creative literature throughout the English speaking world is yet to be fully understood and valued. I for one, greatly appreciate his enthusiastic commitment to placing fresh, untried talent before the reading public.

Stephen Meredith Iball designed the cover for the book with little to go on except the title and a surrealist painting entitled, 'What Next?'. An eye-catching envelope in which to post the story was Stephen's handiwork.

Kathy Austin unravelled grammatical knots and rejigged punctuation throughout the text to ensure the desired intension of each sentence was realised and intelligible. The winter sunshine Down Under is presently assisting with her syntactic recuperation.

Thank you David, Stephen and Kathy for your help in the ultimate realisation this novel.

CONTENTS
CHAPTERS

Part 1

****

A RANDOM WALK INTO THE UNKNOWN

****

Chapter 1 – The Soldier

****

The more I learn about history, the more I feel
astonishingly lucky that I am alive today
when you consider the hell our ancestors lived through.

Dan Snow, Historian & TV Presenter (1978 – and onward)

The Telegraph Magazine 15 April 2017

****

"Checkmate Grandad," whispered Fynn, with the merest hint of amused self-satisfaction playing about his young face.

Magnus Henry, confused by the know-how and confidence of one so young, gave his grandson a lingering look before shaking his little hand and saying, "Super game Fynn. You've now beaten me eight times. But be careful, one of these days I'll win."

There's something pleasing, yet unsettling, about an elderly wise owl being out-manoeuvred on a chessboard by a six-year-old. Behind Magnus's obvious pride in his grandson's ability to play with such self-assurance and skill, there lurked a shadow of unease – an anxiety and self-doubt that may leave many retirees uncertain of their place in the world.

Fynnlo's future, on the other hand, was perfectly clear. He wished to become a champion chess player, a champion soccer player and a champion tennis player – who kept servants and ran a window cleaning business on the side – commendable goals for a youngster that revealed a degree of foresight and conviction not evident in Magnus until he was well into his sixties, a time of life when most such opportunities had long since passed him by.

Magnus was holidaying with his daughter Fenella and her family in Brisbane, Australia, which was also his home town. At that time however, his house was rented while he spent a year or two of retirement revisiting his origins on the Isle of Man. How he came to call Australia home, which is on the far side of the world from where he was brought-up, is a tortuous tale of serendipity and happenstance.

The Isle of Man is a small self-governing island in the middle of the Irish Sea. It's part of the

British Isles, but not of the United Kingdom. Recent archaeological diggings on the Island unearthed evidence of a farming settlement dating back over 8000 years, much earlier than previously thought for agriculture in Europe. For a millennium or more, it was a remote island with insular and superstitious inhabitants of mixed Celtic and Nordic blood. Although there is no indication of Roman settlement, it's difficult to believe that during their four-hundred-year occupation of Britannia, those avaricious land-grabbers didn't send in the assessors to gauge the island's commercial and military possibilities. The Romans, if they arrived at all, may not have been impressed by what they saw, however, the ninth century Nordic Vikings adopted an altogether less apathetic attitude. For these Norse sea wolves, the island was Valhalla in the Irish Sea; so much so, that the island remained a vital part of the Nordic Empire well into the thirteenth century.

The fortunes of the island's native inhabitants, the Manx, have varied throughout history. Presently the local populace is thriving, thanks to offshore finance, insurance, on-line gambling, shipping and aviation registries etc. In the nineteenth century however, after Karl Marx penned his treatise, *Das Kapital*, which was partially informed by the miseries of the Industrial Revolution factory workers in Manchester, a friend of Marx commented, "The Manx rustics are worse off than the white industrial slaves you've observed Karl. Fortunately for them, they're oblivious of the fact."

A century later, during the 1950's, the island still offered limited opportunity for year round employment. Being a summer tourist island meant that residents could hold down two jobs during the holiday season; however, with limited winter employment, many people were obliged to leave the island to find work. For instance, Norfolk provided winter work 'on the sugar beet', processing root vegetables to extract the white death – sugar.

As a child, Magnus often helped out on farms and would have been happy following in his forefathers' footsteps as farmers in the Parish of Kirk Lonan, but without a family farm, and no means of getting one, his fancy faded to a forgotten dream.

Like most children at that time, he had several summer holiday jobs other than revelling in the zesty open air and sunshine of farm life. Two extremes were laundry ironing (a prison with heat and steam), and more successfully, hiring out deckchairs to happy holiday-makers on Douglas promenade (smiles with blue sea and sky). Whilst working at the seaside, a holiday-maker gave Magnus a thin cowboy paperback he'd just finished reading on the beach. This became the first book Magnus read from cover to cover, and initiated the new found and lifelong pleasure of reading. He was then fifteen years of age and had already left school.

Magnus's mother, Margaret Lillian, steered her youngest son away from plumbing and TV maintenance apprenticeships (which would have kept him at home) towards the aspiration of further education. This had the far-reaching consequence of him having to leave the island where tertiary education was unavailable.

Apart from observing what those around him on the island did to earn a living, Magnus remained ignorant of what employment possibilities existed, what job requirements were, or what most professions entailed. Like everybody else, he didn't know what he didn't know, and didn't even know that. In this blithe state of ignorance, he slavishly followed the familiar path towards an assured future of paid education and adventure with the British armed forces, a calling for which he believed he was aptly qualified. Thanks to a mop of bright red hair (a genetic signature that came with his Celtic/Viking blood) he was nearly always charged for action, a trait he considered an obvious prerequisite for a budding soldier.

As a fourteen-year-old newly promoted single-stripe Lance Bombardier in his school's Army Cadet Force, Magnus decided to become an officer cadet with the British Army. Army scholarships were available for technical training at

Welbeck College, followed by military schooling at the Royal Military Academy, Sandhurst. He was comfortable with these prospects, knowing that a mere private from the school cadet contingent of the previous year had been accepted as promising officer material despite his inability to march. Magnus's naive reasoning was that, if somebody who was unable to master disciplined walking was acceptable to the British Army, anyone could get in.

A chance meeting with this older scholarship cadet, who at the time was on leave from Welbeck College, revealed that tuition was not restricted to technical issues alone. Included in the mix were the subtle skills of leadership which included 'officer speak' elocution lessons. This socially segregating system imbued the spoken word an obligatory sense of authority to differentiate between officers and the ranks.

It was widely understood that training in the armed forces would provide a recruit with suitable skills for subsequent employment as a civilian. For instance, consider the stellar career of Adolf Hitler. Throughout the 1920's, the lowly born Hitler enjoyed a meteoric rise from the menial rank of corporal during The Great War, to the exalted post of Chancellor of Germany in little over a decade, even though constrained by Germany's rigid social structure. It should never be forgotten however, that Hitler came to power with a significant advantage over his rivals. He believed he enjoyed a foreknowledge of events, thanks to the psychic skill of the Swiss-born astrologer, Karl Ernst Krafft.

Many Manx families of Magnus's generation had connections with the Armed Forces having relatives or friends bivouacked around the globe. During the 1950's, Britons were raised on an unremitting diet of war films, cinema newsreels of independence skirmishes throughout the crumbling British Empire, and Territorial Army recruitment drives. And if that wasn't enough to 'stiffen the sinews and summon up the blood' of the recalcitrant few who hadn't been paying attention, there was also the weekly black and white TV fix of *The World at War* or *War at Sea*. Military actions filled the daily newspapers and even the Sabbath wasn't exempt from the relentless militaristic bombardment. The BBC's dedicated armed forces musical request programme, *Two-Way Family Favourites*, wafted through the house while the Sunday joint was being prepared. And to crown it all, the Sword of Damocles of conscription into National Service hung over the heads of all but the flat-footed, the well-connected or those otherwise excused.

To an aspiring Manx youngster, a life of exploration as an Officer Cadet in the British Army was there for the taking. Magnus was deemed fit for service after enduring a week-long medical examination conducted in a World War II wooden military hospital near the English/Welsh border town of Chester, a garrison town since Roman times. Accommodated in the officers' wing of the sprawling single-story maze, the fifteen-year-old hopeful peed into funnelled sample bottles, was tapped by hammers and swallowed countless pills. The attendant nurses weren't dressed in the soft white medical attire of Civvy Street, but tweedy uniforms with heavy cloaks and enormous starched sphinx-like wimples, the whole regalia trimmed with insignia, campaign ribbons and badges of rank.

His first encounter with an expressly army type occurred on arrival in the small, seemingly unoccupied, officers' ward in which he'd been assigned the first bed on the left, next to the entrance. There were five or so beds set on each side of the starkly functional ward. Half-way down the far side of the ward, one bed was screened by pull around curtains.

"Who are you?" An authoritative voice barked whilst Magnus unpacked clothes into a small bedside locker. "And what the blazes are you doing here?"

"McAulay Sir, I'm an applicant for Welbeck College," Magnus replied to the bedraggled head that protruded horizontally from between the curtains of the screened bed opposite, and which sported an impressive Moshe Dayan style black eye patch.

"Good for you," the bedridden warrior boomed. "Been a 'Rupert' over thirty years. Made Brigadier. Been worldwide. Rowed every decent stretch of water in the UK. Damned fine life, the Army. Well looked after. Been in hospital five years in the past eight. Lost this eye on night manoeuvres. One of the chaps let a hawthorn branch go swish – knocked me dashed eye out. Good luck with your application."

With that, the Brigadier's hoary head slowly disappeared into the isolated comfort of the curtained enclosure, as a giant Galapagos tortoise might withdraw into the sanctuary of its shell. And that's the last Magnus saw of that professional soldier, one who may have been happier emptying a Bren gun from the hip than negotiating peace terms with a determined enemy.

All meals were held in the officers' mess, which was an eye-opener to a country boy, even a convivial type with passable table manners. Most accents were terribly clipped, far-back officer-speak that became doubly so when women diners were present. Magnus was the only Welbeck hopeful in the exclusive company of mostly elderly military types but he was treated with courtesy and respect by the diners and the stewards.

Perhaps not unexpectedly, Magnus failed the Welbeck entrance exams, held some weeks later, again near Chester, and was deemed unsuitable officer cadet material. Battling dyslexia, he was at best a stumbling reader, who shone as a world-class creative speller, a skill that could fox those with more conventional literary and grammatical attitudes – such as the conformist military establishment. In truth, his chess playing grandson Fynnlo was a better reader at six than Magnus had been at fifteen, his age when sitting the examinations. His army evaluation report may have read: "Not the ideal candidate to be writing communiqués or reading out orders in dire situations; best rejected to minimise casualties on both sides".

Following the army entrance exams, the aspirants, predominantly from privileged private schools, awaited their fate in a small conference room.

"I've heard that if the interview is cut short, you've botched the papers and you're out on your ear," one of the candidates stated to the apprehensive group.

A well turned-out, straight-backed subaltern escorted individual applicants into an adjacent room for interview and appraisal.

"Mr Moral," the subaltern called out.

"Not Moral Sir – Morrell," the stylish, self-assured hopeful remonstrated, before being escorted to his interview by the smirking junior officer.

When 'Mr McAulay' was called, Magnus followed the subaltern into a stark room that veritably crackled with razor-edged military crispness. The chief interrogator, a stiff, square-shouldered Colonel, who was also Principal of Welbeck College, sat behind a table with the rest of the assessment team to his left; a mighty force to grill the fifteen-year-old schoolboy sitting in the hot seat at the focal point of the gathering.

All present were impeccably attired in finely tailored khaki service uniforms, resplendent with brilliant white lanyards, red and gold epaulettes, waxed and highly polished Sam Browne leathers and glistening brass paraphernalia, together with a plethora of colourful campaign ribbons, decorations and insignia. The panel's batmen must have worked well into the night to present so impressive a turnout.

"Well McAulay, your maths leaves a lot to be desired." the 'Colonel Blimp' broadcast forcefully, peering hard at the boy over half-moon glasses, before scrutinising the papers in front of him.

This confused Magnus, as technical subjects, particularly maths, were his favourites, at which he was normally competent, and occasionally shone. 'If I've failed maths, heaven knows what a pig's ear

I made of the English and General Knowledge papers,' he mused to himself with concern.

"Here, factorise this equation," his interrogator challenged in a plummy staccato.

Written on a paper was what Magnus understood to be the algebraic equation for the difference of two squares, but raised to the power four, something he'd never come across before. Unsettled by the intimidating and overbearing atmosphere, and without time to think or ask questions, the answer he proposed to the algebraic riddle was incorrect. So that was that; no army education or officer cadetship in prospect for Magnus.

"Woeful State education," the Welbeck Principal commented to his colleagues, leaning forward, kneading his brow. "But what else do you expect from these people? Thank you McAulay, that'll be all."

Magnus left the room without saying a word, but seethed internally: "These people! But what are you Sir, if not a sanctioned school bully in fancy dress?"

Humiliated and ashamed, Magnus did not return to the waiting room to join the other candidates who would guess at a rejection by his hangdog demeanour and the short duration of the interview. Instead he retreated to the back of the canvas-covered army wagon, to endure the journey back to the Station Hotel, where the applicants had been billeted, and from there onward home.

At Chester railway station he met a fellow applicant, the amiable Mr Morrell.

"Hello McAulay," he called out. "How the blazes did you fare in that shemozzle?"

"Not well I'm afraid," he replied sheepishly. "What about you?"

"OK… I believe," he said. "Don't worry if you weren't accepted. It's only the blasted army after all. Good luck."

And with that he waved goodbye and moved off to catch a train back to his boarding school and the prospect of a professional education and commission in Her Majesty's Armed Forces.

Magnus admired Mr Morrell's panache and suspected that had they studied together at Welbeck and Sandhurst, they might have become good friends.

The Army medical was held several weeks before the entrance examinations in the early months of 1959 and for the intervening period Magnus returned home to attend school as it was his crucial final year when the GCE examinations were held.

It was winter and, outside the wooden barracks-like hospital where the medical was held, the air was sharp and the pavement was covered in thick, uneven shards of ice. Chilled to the bone,

Magnus waited for the bus to Birkenhead where he would stay overnight with his maternal grandparents. The following morning he'd catch the ferry across the River Mersey (together with the late-to-work/early home, bowler-hatted, deck-strutting, Liverpool businessmen), to board the *King Orry*, a Manx boat, to sail home to the Isle of Man.

While waiting outside the military hospital for the bus, Magnus observed the light road traffic passing by. One car in particular caught his attention, not because it was a new black and chrome 3.8 Jaguar or a drop-head, apple green Riley piloted by a daredevil blond beauty wearing goggles, but because the 'sit-up-and-beg' Ford Popular had driven past in both directions before pulling up at the bus stop.

"Where are you going?" the young driver called out cheerfully.

"Birkenhead," Magnus replied.

"That's where I'm heading. Get in. I'll drive you there," the man replied smiling.

The fact that the car had passed by several times made Magnus look hard and long at the driver before declining the offer of a lift, which, had it been on the Isle of Man, where hitchhiking was commonplace and safe, he would have gladly accepted.

"Come ahead, get in," the motorist insisted. "If I give you a lift, it'll save you time and money."

"No thanks," he declined. "The bus will be here in a minute, and I have a return ticket."

"Get in," the driver insisted with a menacing edge to his voice. "You'll be safe with me. Get in."

"No thank you," Magnus stated firmly, raising his hand to signal the bus that had just come into view.

Some years later, Magnus recognised the driver's face from a police mug shot on TV. It may have been Ian Brady, who, with Myra Hindley, was convicted of murdering five young people during the 1960's. The depraved team, collectively known as the Moors Murderers, disposed of their victims on the wasteland of Saddleworth Moor.

That wasn't the only nasty surprise associated with being absent from school to take the Army medical. When Magnus arrived back at Douglas High School he discovered that his name had been left off the GCE Art examination list. As he'd topped his class in both mock art tests, which provided a gauge to the pupil's final examination prospects, the disqualification was totally unreasonable and unexpected. His appeal to the school Head Master proved futile. Because of tensions between Magnus and the art teacher, he left school with one less certificate than should have been the case. It's probable that having an additional subject, specifically art, would have made little difference throughout his erratic working life. This episode reinforced Magnus's growing belief that many in authority frequently abuse the privilege their office afforded. This understanding ultimately crystallised into a lifelong wariness of powerful, inconsistent and self-righteous officialdom.

The seeds for Magnus's guarded approach to authority were sown well before the art teacher denied him entry for the school leaving certificate. Three years earlier, he and two friends were hauled before the bench for several childish misdemeanours which included lifting a handful of chocolate bars from the ice cream kiosk next to a gypsy fortune teller's booth in Groudle Glen (a tourist's woodland). The police inadvertently legitimised the summer trader's exaggerated claim on the charge sheet which stated that a box containing a gross of chocolate bars had been stolen. A good 'result' for the police efficiency and prosecution statistics, and an unexpected windfall profit from unsold, discoloured end of season stock for the retailer whose potentially fraudulent insurance claim was no doubt paid in full. All the adults benefited from the conspiracy at the expense of the twelve-year-old lads whose villainous stupidity promoted the profit making scam.

For their scandalous behaviour, the three sweet-toothed delinquents were subjected to the full might of The Law. The twelve year olds were fingerprinted, mug-shot photographed (both full-face and profile) and exposed to a judicial system that favoured corporal punishment. Magistrate 'Bircher' Quayle, or one of his ilk, convicted and sentenced Magnus and a fellow delinquent to be birched.

Curiously, the magnificent building in which Magnus came face to face with the might and impersonal callousness of The Law was one of the finest on the island and had been designed by his great-great uncle and built by his great-great grandfather. The courthouse, originally built as the island's headquarters for The Independent Order of Odd Fellows was but one of many famous architectural triumphs the nineteenth century entrepreneurial Robinson duo built in the island's capital, Douglas. It's interesting to conjecture upon how the ghostly manifestations of Magnus's illustrious forebears might have reacted to the ignominy of their direct descendant being debased and flayed in a bleak basement beneath one of their most admired buildings.

Before the punishment was carried out, a policeman thrashed the birch rods across a table top in front of the boys so the youngsters could contemplate upon the excruciating pain which shortly would be coming their way. One by one, the terrified children were forced to bend over a prison cell bunk to be lashed on their bare buttocks with a bundle of four feet long birch rods wielded by a burly policeman with his shirtsleeves rolled-up to better lay it on.

It was never confirmed, although Magnus thought it may have been the case, that the notary bearing witness to the punishment in a prison cell where the flogging was inflicted, was none other than the sentencing magistrate himself. Whilst the lashes were being inflicted, this sweaty-skinned witness stood half hidden in a shadowy corner of the dingy prison cell nervously playing with the loose change deep in his trouser pocket. In attendance also was the school doctor who served a dual purpose; he was witness to the flogging, but was also conveniently on hand in case the overly zealous flaying caused gashes in the children's skin that required medical attention.

Magnus's immunity from social ridicule and humiliation through the miscreants' identity being withheld from the newspaper report wasn't extended to one of the other indicted children in the courtroom line-up that morning. In addition to the barbarous punishment inflicted on him in the prison cell, he was hauled before the entire assembly of his Manx private school peers for public chastisement and degradation. Not content with the lashing he received at the hands of the police, the headmaster thought it apt to mete out additional punishment for wreaking dishonour upon so hallowed an institution as his school.

Magnus's partner in crime was given six of the best as an inducement to behave more gentlemanly in future. After being pilloried in front of his fellow pupils, rehabilitation was impossible. No matter what he did, nor how hard he tried, he was never able to live down the scandalous public shaming he suffered at his private, fee-paying school where pupils were being groomed as potential leaders of the British Empire. Twenty years later, during the 1970's he lobbied the European Court of Human Rights to pressurise Tynwald, the Manx Parliament, to rescind the laws that allowed miscreant children to be flogged and demeaned for minor infringements of The Law.

Birching was the rule of the day into the early 1980's at Eton College, one of England's oldest and most revered schools, where pupils tend to be the legitimate and not so legitimate off-spring of the aristocracy and the obscenely wealthy. There was however a significant difference between the punishments inflicted within the hallowed halls of Eton College to that enforced in the grimy prison cell on the Isle of Man. At Eton, misbehaving scholars may be subjected to a beating by a learned schoolmaster who could well have been quietly muttering a self-absolving verse in Latin whilst imposing the punishment. The Manx approach was more rustic and parochial; a strapping copper lashed the child criminals, no doubt at the time cursing the fact that he had been singled out to do so.

The Eton method demonstrated significant long term advantages over the Manx technique. Many Etonian alumni did indeed become masters of the British Empire and several have occupied 10 Downing Street as Prime Ministers of Great Britain. So smitten might others of the well-heeled ex-pupils have been by the success of their old school's harsh disciplinary regime that they chose to relive their aspirations at the hands of the dominatrix queen-bee, Claudia the Sting of Ladbroke Grove. This latex lady may well have reduced a ruthless Minister of Defence to a quivering jelly by the cruel smirk playing across her glossy purple lips or eked-out squeals of eye-watering glee from a tight-lipped Tory Peer with a well-aimed snappy flick of her wetly-lubricated red leather thong.

Magnus's miscreant Manx mate didn't fare so well as the born-to-rule Eton-educated defenders of these titillating treats. After an unsettled life, the three times married seeker died alone, unhappy, and far too young.

Chapter 2 – The Cadet

****

I would rather be a rebel than a slave.

Emmeline Pankhurst (1858 – 1929)

Leader of the British suffragettes

****

As an army reject Magnus had to rethink his future … and fast. Scholarship places were eagerly contested and being enthusiastically snapped-up. Fortunately, there was still the Royal Air Force or the Royal Navy, or even the Merchant Navy, to fall back on.

Manx seafarers have always been held in high regard and have long populated the British Merchant and Royal Navies. It was no accident that, two centuries ago, in a single year, twenty-nine slave ships sailing out of Liverpool were under the command of Manx sea captains.

One Manx sea dog, Hugh Crow, in his memoir, *The Life and Times of a Slave Trade Captain*, restated an oft expunged fact that the human cargo transported westward were already enslaved prisoners held captive by the more warlike and powerful African tribes. Captain Crow observed that many slaves enjoyed a better and more secure life working on the sugar cane and cotton plantations of the Caribbean and the Americas than they ever could have expected at the hands of their pitiless African captors. It was also Crow's contention that these slaves were often better treated than many 'white slaves' he'd observed in squalor and servitude throughout the British Isles and on some ships on which he'd served. It's interesting to conjecture why abolitionist, William Wilberforce, so vehemently pursued the cause to stop the slave trade throughout the British Empire, whilst doing little to alleviate the hardship of his countrymen starving to death in filthy hovels within spitting distance of the Houses of Parliament.

The British slave traders, taking the passage known as the Triangular Trade, sailed from England to West Africa to procure slaves, then to the Americas where the human cargo was sold and general cargo was loaded for shipment back to

England. Many Manxmen were eager accomplices in this lucrative traffic as it enriched local lords and ladies, whilst fuelling the illegal 'running trade' (smuggling) which for a generation or two profited all involved, except the British Treasury.

Slave ships, outbound from Liverpool, called at the Isle of Man to load their Guinea cargo of slave trading materials. The Manx ports of Douglas and Peel warehoused and supplied these goods, which included beads, cloth, metal bars, looking glasses, gunpowder, muskets, knives and cutlasses. On the return leg of these trading forays, slave ships, homeward bound from the Caribbean or the Americas, routinely dropped anchor at Manx ports to discharge a quota of their goods that was strangely absent from the ship's cargo manifest. This contraband (cotton, tobacco and rum) was the lifeblood of Manx late eighteenth century commerce.

Captain William Bligh, of *Mutiny on the Bounty* fame, was stationed at the Isle of Man to command HM Sloop *Resolution*. His orders were to prevent contraband entering British territories bordering the Irish Sea by policing Manx coastal waters. The objective of the exercise was to stop the Lords of Man and Manx smugglers picking the pockets of His Majesty's Treasury. During Captain Bligh's command, whilst based at the island capital, Douglas, he met two people who greatly influenced the course of his life – his future wife, Elizabeth Betham, and his nemesis, the HMS *Bounty* mutineer, Fletcher Christian.

Even though those roguish but profitable days of slavery and smuggling are long gone, life at sea still attracts many Manx recruits, including Magnus's maternal grandfather, Alfred Henry. Harry as he was known, wasn't raised by his parents, but a maiden aunt, a common practice in late Victorian times. Rather than joining the family printing business alongside his two brothers, Harry trained as a marine engineer with the Isle of Man Steam Packet Shipping Company sailing to a variety of ports around the Irish Sea. Prior to the outbreak of The Great War in 1914, he ventured deep-sea with Elders and Fyffes, a shipping company which operated a fleet of refrigerated boats trading bananas from the Canary Islands and the Caribbean.

Due to the catastrophic slaughter in Europe during World War I, the lunatics of British High Command ran a successful recruiting campaign in 1916 to deliver tens of thousands more men to German butchery. Patriotic Harry volunteered, swapping the noise and heat of a ship's engine room, for the squalor and whiz-bang depravity of the Western Front trenches. He survived, whilst most around him were massacred. In due course he was reassigned back to the Merchant Navy because so many marine engineers had volunteered to fight the Bosch that essential shipping services were left perilously shorthanded.

With Liverpool his ship's home port, Harry and his wife Agnes Maud were obliged to move from the Celtic/Norse Isle of Man to become residents on Merseyside's Wirral Peninsular in the county of Cheshire, in Saxon England.

On relocating, Agnes Maud was justifiably a touch testy at being denied a vote for representation in Britain's parliament because she was a woman. The gem-sized Isle of Man, which claimed the oldest continuous parliament, Tynwald, was also the first nation to introduce universal suffrage. Manx women had enjoyed political emancipation since the early 1880's, over forty years before Westminster MP's saw the light in Britain's misogynistic Houses of Parliament and granted women the vote for political representation.

Unsurprisingly, Emmeline Pankhurst, the early champion of the British suffragette movement, had more than a hint of fiery Manx blood coursing through her veins; her mother was a Manx girl from Lonan Parish. The first predominantly European community in the world to embrace universal suffrage was also pulsing with Manx blood; the Pitcairn Islanders, descendants of the HMS *Bounty* mutineers, directed by Fletcher Christian, agreed equal rights for all in 1838.

Maud had an inquiring mind, and even supported the introduction of Esperanto as a universal language. In her youth she deliberated upon most Protestant denominations, including the oxymoronically named Christian Scientists. She was initially attracted to this church because the seductive doctrine it championed was that a right-thinking person need never die. The problem with this creed remained that nobody, not even the church's founder, Mary Baker Eddy, could pinpoint with certainty what right-thinking actually was. Maud quickly recognised the flaw in this canon, for no matter what peaks of spiritual purity they attained, members of the congregation kept on dying. She eventually favoured the then widely followed and esteemed Spiritualist Church. Although she never aspired to become a medium herself, the church's psychic pedigree nourished her innately superstitious nature. Maud professed to possess the rare gift of clairvoyance which enabled her to discern apparitions where others saw nothing. Practical outlets for this intuitive engagement with the paranormal were augmented with daily reference to Old Moore's *Almanack* (an astrological year book published in Britain since 1697). Maud mingled her psychic gift with events foretold in the almanac and guidance from the *Daily Mail* newspaper's horoscope column, to achieve a reputation for being able to conjure-up an understanding of future events. Her most successful predictions were forecasting the afternoon's weather, which tended to agree with the BBC's meteorological reports.

Family mythology had it that Maud was a direct descendant of King Kelly of Peel, a noble lineage of unsullied Manx blood. On English soil, she was an independent but frustrated emancipated woman who ensured her three daughters received the benefits of the finest education then available. Despite this practical, common sense approach to life, Maud's Manx blood bequeathed a deeply superstitious nature that was impossible to suppress.

Gypsy wives peddling handmade copper wrapped, willow or hazel wood clothes pegs door-to-door were valued guests in Maud's house. Over a pot of tea, she would cross the gypsy's palm with silver as inducement for the true reason for the gathering – not the sale of clothes pegs, of which she had a bucketful, but the shamanistic wonders of soothsaying. Maud would delight in the dark-eyed fortune-teller's readings of the unique lines on her taut palm, the clairvoyant's divination of random patterns of tea leaves at the bottom of her china teacup, and crucially, the seer's astral interpretation of her psychic aura. What a gift! What a thrill! What a bargain! A guaranteed three-way cross-referenced golden future and all for an outlay of only a half-crown.

One of Magnus's primary school class mates was the exotic sultry-eyed Laura, the daughter of the flamboyantly draped, slow moving, gypsy fortune-teller who exercised her celestial mesmerism at the Onchan Head fairground. He had never crossed Laura's palm with silver, as he'd never owned a half-crown, but he would have, if he could have.

Some years later, when in his teens, Magnus had reason to examine his own superstitious inheritance more closely. The half-brother of Magnus's school mate, Denis, had been killed in a road accident so the two friends endeavoured to make contact with the crash victim across the 'Big Divide'. Denis's grandmother was a stalwart member of the Spiritualist Church and an authentic medium who, surprisingly, was predisposed to act as the psychic conduit at a séance. The congregation of three sat around a small polished topped table on which the marquetry alphabet, numerals and the words 'yes' and 'no' were inlaid in a circle on a true believer's talking board. All three rested their index finger on the top of a centrally placed, pre-warmed, water glass. To evoke the supernatural world, they sang from hymn sheets during which the self-conscious sixteen-year-old lads had trouble stifling laughter and keeping straight faces. As the third hymn reached its crescendo however, the atmosphere in the room changed subtly. Kim,

Denis's mongrel dog, which had been contentedly resting in front of the open coal fire, suddenly sprang up, wide-eyed and scurried out of the room with its head down, ears back and its tail between its legs. At the same instant the glass began to whizz around the table causing the blood to drain from the lads' startled faces. Contact was made, questions asked, messages spelled out, and doubts challenged. Magnus was pleased that neither Sitting Bull nor Black Hawk, nor any other of the popular red-skin chiefs was evoked as a channel to the *Great Spirit World*. That evening all witnesses from beyond-the-grave identified themselves as deceased relatives of those present. Magnus attended one more séance after this episode and, instead of remaining a vocal sceptic about his grandmother's spiritualist beliefs; he adopted an open-minded attitude towards mystical phenomena, including contact from those passed on.

Whilst Maud was busy calling upon her paranormal powers to predict the weather or future football pools winning teams, her husband Harry was criss-crossing the Atlantic Ocean. He spent most of his working life at sea, and nearly died there, something Maud feared but never foretold.

Just after midnight on 30th November 1940, Harry's blacked-out cargo ship, SS *Aracataca*, whilst steaming in convoy across the North Atlantic Ocean on a zigzag course at 13 knots about 230 nautical miles west of Rockall, was torpedoed by the German U-Boat, U-101. This wasn't a clean 'kill' as seen at the cinema. The 28-year-old submarine commander, Kapitänleutnant Ernst Mengeren, was obliged to 'Los!' three precious torpedoes into the ship's hull before her engine room boiler exploded, sending the *Aracataca* with her cargo of 1600 tons of grapefruit and bananas below the waves to Davy Jones Locker. In the midnight blackness, all 67 petrified crew abandoned ship into four lifeboats. Harry survived three days adrift in an open lifeboat battling mountainous seas and the freezing temperatures of a North Atlantic winter. From this horrific ordeal he was lucky to have suffered nothing more than frostbitten toes, and in all probability, a shortened life span. He and a quarter of the ship's crew in one of the lifeboats were rescued by the M/S *Potaro*, a free French merchantman, outbound for South America. The survivors were put ashore at Buenos Aires on Christmas Day. Thirty-seven of Harry's fellow crewmen weren't so lucky. Two lifeboats and all aboard disappeared, lost at sea, where they'd be picked over by the crabs and bizarre sea creatures that feast in the murky depths of the Atlantic Ocean.

In keeping with the then 'generous' maritime terms of employment, all pay stopped at the moment they abandoned ship. Whilst lazily lounging in lifeboats, the frozen and soaking wet survivors were no longer working on behalf of their employer, but for themselves, trying desperately to save their own lives, a pastime in which the shipping company had little, if any, financial interest.

Harry's family found out about the sinking of the SS *Aracataca*, not via official notification, but by accident. Elsie, Maud and Harry's eldest daughter, saw the headlines, '*Aracataca* Torpedoed' in a fellow bus passenger's newspaper, *The Liverpool Echo*. Needless to say, there was no telling what had befallen the crew; nobody knew whether they were alive or dead. Elsie's father could have been blown to pieces, burned alive, drowned, or frozen to death, as was the demise of many whose ships were torpedoed and sunk crossing the Atlantic Ocean in mid-winter during World War II.

Having succumbed to tales of life at sea as a continuous round of wine, women and song, Magnus's elder brother, James Arthur Radcliffe, chose to follow in his grandfather's footsteps to become a marine engineer. Magnus couldn't understand why his brother fell for this line, as the story-teller was a friend's stepfather whose wartime exploits were hardly a recommendation for a life on the ocean waves. This jolly tar's Royal Navy experience, after the Japanese sank his warship, HMS *Prince of Wales*, somewhere in the South

China Sea, spent the rest of the war starving in a Burma Railway slave labour camp, where he'd spent punishment time nailed through his fingers to a tree as entertainment for his Japanese captors. But a seafarer's life was James Arthur Radcliffe's destiny. During the spring of 1959, he signed on to train as an Engineer Officer Cadet with Elder Dempster, another Liverpool based shipping company. James's employer plied its trade between Europe and the former slave ports of West Africa, historically regarded as 'The White Man's Grave' because of its inhospitable climate, deadly diseases, and poor sanitation.

Following the demise of the British Merchant Navy during the 1980's, James was obliged to sail as a Chief Engineer for whichever foreign flagged shipping company would give him a berth. He remained at sea until ill health forced premature retirement in his early sixties.

Tainted by the ignominy of his failure to become a budding Field Marshall Montgomery in the British Army, Magnus dithered over a panicky and late application to train as an Engineer Officer Cadet in the merchant navy. He sat selection exams aboard the modern cargo/passenger liner, the Indian Lascar and Goan crewed *City of Port Elizabeth*, moored on the River Thames in London. This time destiny smiled on him and he was successful in finding a sponsor for further education and training with Ellerman Lines.

One month after his sixteenth birthday, Magnus left the Isle of Man to commence his cadetship in South Shields, a seafaring town at the mouth of the River Tyne, in the north-east of England. The training course comprised two years at Marine College, followed by twelve months of work and study aboard cargo ships trading worldwide. During his year at sea, he sailed nearly twice around the world, before returning to college for a final year's study.

South Shields rewarded Magnus with his first taste of romance, although it didn't last very long. Aisha, a dark eyed beauty he met at Bailey's Jazz Club, was a shapely and intelligent Palestinian Geordie. One evening she arrived at the club with her two formally dressed elder brothers in tow. They were there to give Magnus, their sister's friends and the club the once over, and report back to the family. Even though everybody enjoyed the evening, from then on, Aisha never appeared at the club, nor played any part in Magnus's life again.

Like many young people, once set free from a domestic routine and parental influence, his life became a tussle of resolve between the pursuit of disciplined study and hedonism. Initially the self-indulgence was grabbed with both hands, until fate intervened to pitch him onto a studious path to pass the final examinations necessary to proceed with the cadetship.

During a Mechanics of Machines lecture, whilst the students were heads-down working, the lecturer, Mr Underwood, whispered in Magnus's ear, "The College Principal wishes to see you right now."

Leaving the class to continue its work, the pair walked in silence along the empty corridors to the Principal's office, a place best avoided.

"After your recent behaviour McAulay, I'm considering expelling you from The College," the Principal, Dr Stoddart, stated firmly. "Have you anything to say?"

"It wasn't my fault. I didn't want a fight. I didn't start the fight. I was trying to stop a fight," Magnus replied in shock, then explained in detail what had transpired, finishing, "…and everybody knows Flash is a nasty bully, especially when drunk."

"But you pleaded guilty," stated the Principal who moonlighted as a magistrate.

"Yes," Magnus stated. "That was the advice I got, and I think the lawyer was right."

"Why plead guilty if you say you were innocent?" quizzed the Principal uncomprehendingly.

"I expected my pals to come forward and explain what happened, but none did, so the lawyer argued that it was impossible to know how the ruckus started unless a full hearing was held," he explained, "...and I've got no money to pay for that. The obvious solution was to cut my losses by pleading guilty."

"But now you'll have a conviction recorded against you," stated the bemused Principal.

"I'm sorry, but I'll just have to wear that," he replied, thinking to himself, 'If I'm expelled I'll be punished twice for something that wasn't my fault and my education will be up the spout as well.'

The College Principal sat back and looked at Magnus for a considerable time, then asked, "How much did the lawyer charge for advice and representation?"

"A guinea," Magnus replied.

After a further long pause the Principal continued, "After what you've explained, I've reconsidered your expulsion from college, but if I have to deal with you again, you'll be out on your ear. That's all."

Back in the empty corridor Mr Underwood said quietly, "I think you just taught our tame magistrate a salient lesson there McAulay. From now on, keep your nose clean, there's a good lad."

Adhering to this sound counsel was easy once ousted from the lodgings where the brawl took place and which he shared with his partying friends. The move proved to be a blessing in disguise. In new digs, he found himself in the company of affable, diligent students, whose industry and generosity of spirit rubbed off, inspiring him to work hard and pass the final exams.

The diploma Magnus attained at marine college was precisely that which he would have worked for had he been successful in gaining entry to Welbeck College with the British Army. The qualifications may have been the same, but had he been awarded the credentials from Welbeck College his persona and future life would have been very different. There can be little doubt that military discipline would have reset many of Magnus's social attitudes and remodelled his appearance and demeanour into an army stereotype. Had he failed to achieve the prerequisites for officer training at Sandhurst, it's probable that Magnus would have been let go – a discard who'd learned to speak confidently in a clear, well-enunciated voice, having had the guttural slur of an exaggerated Scouse accent, which at the time had been popular at his school, washed out of his mouth with a large slab of Welbeck boarding school soap.

Magnus was occasionally mystified as to why providence seemed to intervene at crucial moments in his life by artfully slipping him a wildcard that transformed a losing hand into an unbeatable royal flush. Perhaps it was written in the stars that at some point his life would take on some purpose and meaning. Then again, perhaps he made his own luck. After all he was, like everybody else, the star acting out his own play.

Chapter 3– The Mariner

****

We all see it.
That don't make it real.

Herman Melville (1819 – 1891)

The Manxman, a sailor, Moby Dick

****

At sea, one had to look the part. It was required to be outfitted with all the trappings of an Engineer Officer Cadet. These Magnus purchased from one of many cluttered and gloomy Liverpool gents' outfitters specialising in maritime regalia.

Shipboard life called for three distinct uniforms. Most costly was a double-breasted, brass buttoned, black doeskin uniform with lapel insignia and a badged peaked cap similar to that worn by officers in the Royal Navy, but with Merchant Navy purple-backed gold-wired badging. This uniform was worn when sailing in the world's temperate zones. Uniform whites were adopted when entering tropical waters. The two white outfits consisted of short-sleeved shirts with breast pockets and gold-wired shoulder epaulettes, knee-length shorts, long socks and white canvas leather-soled shoes, and finally, white covers for the crown of the peaked cap. The workplace get-up was white overalls and work boots for use in the ship's engine room. The final item to complete the work-a-day wardrobe was a hussif (sewing kit), an essential accessory for seafarers that had been so for hundreds of years. The complete regalia set him back two month's pay, and that was before he sailed deep-sea.

It wasn't only appearances that needed to be spruced-up to meet the required standard of the officers' dining saloon; a sailor's immune system also needed a booster. Before sailing to foreign parts, Magnus was vaccinated with a cocktail of potions to fend off a plethora of deadly diseases. He was pleased to benefit from the years of research into tetanus, cholera, yellow fever, typhoid and smallpox, diseases which killed millions in the third world countries with whom Ellerman Lines traded.

Magnus's maiden voyage was aboard the diesel-powered *City of Swansea* which sailed from Merseyside to India via the Mediterranean Sea, Suez Canal and Aden, a one-time strategic coalbunkering port for the British Empire. In Aden, some of the crew purchased half-priced, black market Indian Rupees from the bumboat traders who boarded ship to conduct business. Few of the Lascar or Goan crew bought bundles of Rupees, because they had already converted their meagre pay into gold sovereigns in Liverpool. Importing gold into India was illegal, so the smuggled sovereigns commanded premium rates when sold on the Indian black market. One ill-fated Goan steward had his entire twelve-month savings pocketed by a lucky Indian Customs Officer who discovered the seaman's stash of gold sovereigns hidden within the contents of a sugar bowl.

Throughout the trip, Magnus's daily routine was to work two, four-hour engine room watches. The seven-day-a-week, 24-hour cycle started at midnight (0000hrs) with the first watch; the middle watch followed at 0400hrs; and the morning watch commenced at 0800hrs finishing at midday, from which time the cycle was repeated. Magnus usually worked with the Second Engineer on the middle watches (0400-0800hrs and 1600-2000hrs) when trading coastally. Deep-sea, his working day was split between the engine room in the mornings and college correspondence study during the afternoons.

The outbound cargo included a racehorse which was housed in a temporary wooden stall on the aft deck. Rusty, the Deck Officer Cadet, was kept busy feeding and caring for the animal until it was off-loaded in India. One morning the daily routine of shipboard life was unexpectedly cheered by Rusty's howls of shock and pain. The down-in-the-mouth seasick nag had bitten Rusty on the neck while he was mucking-out its box.

The ship docked at Karachi and Bombay and lay at anchor in the small port of Vasco de Gama on the coast of what had been the Portuguese colony of Goa. Magnus was so stunned at witnessing the obscenity of social deprivation and inequity in the coastal cities of the Indian subcontinent that he hoped never to return.

On the voyage back to Europe three memorable incidents occurred. The first was the near sinking of the Russian bulk carrier that followed immediately behind the *City of Swansea* in the north bound convoy through the Suez Canal. The damaged ship took on so much water that her deck was awash and had she not been beached off-channel in the Bitter Lakes (part of the Suez Canal), the ship could have sunk, blocking one of the world's busiest shipping channels.

The second incident happened whilst Magnus's ship battled mountainous seas in the Bay of Biscay whilst corkscrewing and surfing past a battered, straight-funnelled Liberty ship. During World War II, 2,710 Liberty ships were prefabricated across America and assembled at shipyards along the eastern seaboard. They were built to transport essential war supplies of munitions, fuel and food across the Atlantic Ocean to the besieged British. The ships had a very short life expectancy because 'wolf packs' of German U-Boats lined up to blast Allied ships out of the water as they steamed in convoy across the Atlantic Ocean.

The rust-bucket Liberty ship was a miracle of survival, so under-powered she slid backwards as the massive swell moved beneath her aged hull. The ship's existence wasn't so much a testament to the vessel's exceptional durability as to the age-old maxim that some ship owners send sailors to sea in death-traps, so long as there's profit to be had.

The final and most pleasing event happened a few days later after the storm had blown itself out leaving the sea relatively calm. Following a message from the deck officer on watch, Magnus exchanged the cacophonous racket of the excruciatingly hot engine room for the cool fresh air of the wing bridge and was astonished at the sight that greeted him. As far as could be seen – forward, aft, port and starboard – the sea was full of dolphins bearing north. Not pods of a dozen or so each, but a shoal that may have held tens of thousands – an unforgettable sight, about which, when later spoken of, most people remain sceptical.

In January 1963, Magnus joined the steam turbine powered, semi-refrigeration ship, *City of Winchester*, outbound for Australia. She sailed from Merseyside, took on fuel oil bunkers at Las Palmas, then headed south for Durban, in apartheid South Africa. Off the coast of Angola, the Lascar deck serang (Indian bosun) was crushed beneath a bulky cargo hatch-door from which he'd removed the hinge pins, allowing the door to fall as the ship rolled. He died of his injuries several days later. The Lascar crew refused to allow their headman to be buried at sea, which was the fate of most European crew who die deep-sea, so the ship altered course to set the body ashore in Walvis Bay, South West Africa, later to become the independent state of Namibia.

When sailing by Cape Town, Magnus escaped the hot and humid engine room to work in the fresh air on deck. In the bright sunshine, with Table Mountain as the backdrop, he witnessed a never-to-be-forgotten sight. With mighty force, a sleek, black and white whale breached the ocean surface to soar full-length into the warm air before gravity regained control to send the leviathan crashing back below the waves.

Gravity remains an unsolved riddle, even though everything exists within its orbit. Science believes it to be the force that bends space-time, ignites stars, forms galaxies, and holds the solar system in place. Magnus knew it to be a force of nature that held his feet on the deck and prevented the 'flying' whale jetting ever upward into outer space. He was often heartened to realise that, in a world awash with technical experts, there persists something as commonplace as gravity which remains an elusive secret, not fully understood by a single living soul. Perhaps gravity remains the most all-pervading, yet opaque, of the 'known unknowns'.

The final African ports of call for the *City of Winchester* before heading east for Australia were Beira and Lourenço Marques in Portuguese Mozambique.

"We'll be out of touch with land for the next two weeks," stated the Geordie Second Engineer to Magnus. "If you have any medical issues you'd better get them attended to now, before we sail."

"Strange you should ask Sec," Magnus replied. "In the past few days, eating toast or anything hard hurts my gums."

He was sent to a Portuguese colonial medical centre and there learned that he'd contracted a gum rotting complaint possibly from smoking the disgusting, nicotine-loaded, saltpetre impregnated, duty-free ship cigarettes. On the other hand, it could have been the traditional and agonising tooth loosening scourge of mariners over the centuries, scurvy.

Once again providence chose to intervene on his behalf, but only in the nick of time. Had the gum-burning solution to cure the ailment not been prescribed, it's probable the ship's alcoholic purser (and acting medic) would have had to extract all Magnus's teeth, without anaesthetic or antibiotics, before they sighted the Australian coast.

In some quarters, during the 1930's, it was regarded as a chic 21st birthday present to have all one's teeth removed and replaced by a made-to-measure set of false perfect pearlies. Spirited application of the prescribed gum-burning solution allowed Magnus to forego this once fashionable idiocy.

The *City of Winchester* routinely traded between Australia and the east coast of the USA and Canada. These were her home waters and members of the crew who regularly sailed aboard the ship had friends in most Australian ports on whom to call, whilst the newcomers to the trading route spiced-up shipboard life by inviting young nurses aboard for parties. Nearly all of Magnus's meagre salary went in supporting these lively get-togethers.

The ship was designed to carry both dry and refrigerated cargo. In Brisbane she loaded large consignments of frozen lamb and goat carcases bound for Jamaica. In the early 1960's there was no containerisation, so the frozen meat had to be manhandled from the refrigerated abattoir store into nets to be hoisted aboard using the ship's derricks. The stevedores who did this work were dressed from head to foot in thick brown felt overalls, gloves, boots, and Russian Army style head coverings with cheek flaps. When the bulkily dressed labours emerged from the icebox store into the tropical heat carrying frozen goat carcase they gave-off billowing clouds of white vapour as though they may have been a tribe of smouldering Abominable Snowmen returning from a chilly but successful hunt.

It's mystifying how the mind may selectively cull and rehash experience. Magnus's only clear recollections of the numerous ports his ship put into along the eastern seaboard of the United States and Canada were the many bridges they sailed beneath, none however, more impressive than Australia's Sydney Harbour Bridge. Most explorations, including days of sightseeing in New York and Montréal, had slipped Magnus's mind. He did however have one enduring memory of New York. A photograph on page two of a tabloid newspaper showed a murdered gangster dangling out of the driver's car door; he had five bullets in the head, the sixth bullet missed and embedded itself in the wall of a bank across the street. The gruesome snap nestled comfortably behind the image of Pope John

XXIII whose smiling face covered page one; the Pontiff also died the previous day.

Another vivid memory of the USA was the skull and crossbones sign in a Savannah, Georgia, post office which read: *Beware! Moonshine Kills*.

Brisbane was the first port of call in Australia after the long return voyage across the Pacific Ocean from the USA. In-order to recommence college studies back in South Shields, Magnus and a fellow cadet, Nigel, had to sign-on aboard a homeward-bound ship. The new ship, the *City of Perth*, was berthed in Melbourne, 1,500 miles away. Their transfer required the wonderful overnight sleeper train journeys from Brisbane to Sydney, then onwards the following night to Melbourne.

The young travel agent who arranged the trip and saw the two cadets safely aboard the train at South Brisbane Railway Station was John Brew, an Australian with Manx forebears who, through an inconceivable sequence of events, would later reappear in Magnus's life as his brother-in-law.

Magnus's shipmate came from a musical family. His parents had met during the 1930's aboard the luxury trans-Atlantic liner, the *Empress of Britain*, aboard which his mother played the piano and his father the violin. Prior to a seaboard life, Nigel's mother had been a piano accompanist at the silent films, at a time when live music was used to enrich the audiences' emotional response to the action on screen.

The return trip to Europe from Australia started badly. Life aboard the *City of Perth* was staggeringly uncomfortable as the 8,000-ton ship pounded and shuddered through immense ocean swells across the Great Australian Bight. When the ship passed over the crest of an unusually mountainous lump of water, it surfed down its back side to smash into the trough below. At the base, beneath the enormous wall of salt water sprayed skyward by the cleaving bow, the ship bounced, juddered and groaned alarmingly. There was no respite; no sooner had the vessel righted herself than she was heaved aloft by the relentless onslaught of the next mighty surge of green water which started the roller-coaster ride all over again.

During excessively heavy weather, it's not unknown for the steelwork of unseaworthy, badly designed or poorly constructed ships to be ripped apart causing the vessel to founder and sink. Long legal actions often result, and may be difficult to resolve when evidence is hidden beneath the sea where the only eye witnesses have long since become fish food.

An unscheduled landfall was necessary to put ashore a gravely injured seaman at the former whaling port of Albany, Western Australia. A Lascar donkeyman suffered terrible steam burns to his upper body, head and arms while attending to the main engine boilers. During the daily soot-blowing procedure, a drain-cock flange on a high pressure steam line failed, jetting superheated steam over the hapless crewman. Magnus arrived on the turbine control platform as the injured Indian staggered from behind the starboard boiler. His shirt and most of his vest had been blown away. His normally slicked-back hair was standing on end. His scorched face was soot-black except for two terrified white eyes and a horribly gaping purple mouth. It was as though he'd been smoking a trick cigar that had exploded with mighty force. The brown skin of his forearms had melted away exposing seared, red-raw flesh. Most shocking of all was the way he walked and groaned as he went. He held his arms arched-out from his sides and moved with great care in a rolling gait, following the ship's progress. All was slow-motion, lest contact with the blisteringly hot steel surroundings scuffed off more cooked flesh.

"I doubt he'll live long", the Second Engineer muttered to nobody in particular. "It doesn't take much to finish these people off. They give up too easy".

Later, in Port Said, Egypt, the ship's Captain received notice that the injured donkeyman had been transferred to a specialist burns hospital in Perth, and it seemed probable he'd pull through.

Ironically, the ship's high pressure boiler pipework had undergone a successful 'hammer test' insurance survey whilst berthed in Melbourne. It may be that the heavy-handed, blacksmith-style safety inspection weakened the rusty flange enough for it to blow off and barbeque the donkeyman a day or two later.

Back in South Shields the old partying gang was reunited in revelry, with Magnus an active member full of added gusto and self-destructive zest. Study was half-hearted and lectures missed. Life spiralled downwards into a pattern of immature selfishness and general disinterest. Daily lubrication at the local pub kept him and his mates immune to the inevitable consequences of their reckless behaviour.

An acrimonious separation from Ellerman Lines was the result of Magnus and his colleagues unwisely exposing their extortionate landlady to the arbitrational dictates of a Rent Tribunal, an action their employer vehemently objected to.

After a light-hearted spell as a jobbing painter amongst the mainly female workforce of Wrights Biscuit Factory in South Shields, there followed a miserable few months in the dole queue on the Isle of Man. Magnus gleaned a modicum of self-respect and independence by landing a summer job delivering beer around the Island for Mannington's Brewery.

While dressing for work one morning, he noticed a muscular and healthy-looking individual looking back at him from the bedroom mirror. He was surprised at how the heavy work of humping beer crates and rocking hefty barrels of bitter beer on to their chocked place on wooden stillage had reshaped his body, and that was regardless of the generous quantity of free beer that was drunk and enjoyed at each pub visited.

Cast as a failure at nineteen, but instinctively the optimist who may eventually learn from his mistakes, Magnus continued to seek sponsored education that could lead to worthwhile employment. After several months of frustration awaiting a positive reply to job applications from the twice daily postal deliveries, he received an offer.

His potential employer was Christian Salvesen, a company that had been one of the biggest whaling companies in the world, with a blubber rendering slaughterhouse located on the isolated and desolate island of South Georgia. This icy and windswept hell was located in the South Atlantic Ocean approximately due east of Cape Horn and a mere 12 degrees of latitude north of the Antarctic Circle.

He attended an interview with Salvesen's at Leith, the sea port for Scotland's capital, Edinburgh.

There he was offered the continuation of his marine engineering cadetship.

"I've discussed your behaviour with Ellerman, and agree with them that you've acted foolishly and irresponsibly. You were in South Shields to study marine engineering, not fight social issues," stated the portly and humourless Salvesen's Marine Superintendent, trying to stamp his hairy-nostril authority on Magnus's forehead. He continued, "Even considering this, Salvesen's is prepared to give you a second chance, for which you should show eternal gratitude".

"Oh yes Sir, I will," Magnus replied sincerely. "I'm most grateful. And you won't regret putting your faith in me."

****

I had to laugh at this obsequious outburst. However, in all fairness, there can be little doubt Magnus meant it when he said it.... but I doubted it would last.

Sorry, but I'm forgetting my manners. Let me introduce myself. I'm Magnus's ever present inner voice, sneeringly ridiculed by sceptics as 'the ghost within the meme machine'. I'm his spark of life, the scintillating burst that flashed into existence at the moment of conception to animate his physical and psychic being. I'm his unique life force made manifest with the fusion of his parents' quarantined essences. I colonise each cell of Magnus's body to energise the 150 trillion mitochondria that power his subconscious mind from where memory is configured to illuminate consciousness. I complete his being as keeper of his lifelong self-plex in which is preserved every thought, dream and sensory action of our co-dependent existence. I retain these remembrances which are ultimately passed over within our psychic aura into the ever-growing pool of collective experience. I'm both the observer and archivist of every aspect of Magnus's being and as such know him better than he chooses to know himself; in this regard he's little different to most people, in that he lives within the delusional constraints of habitual behaviour.

As a 19-year-old, Magnus almost exclusively inhabits the purely material world, although occasionally he becomes entangled within, and is confused by, aspects of his elusive transcendent nature. Even though I'm with him every nanosecond of every hour of every day, know all his beliefs and secrets, he is all but ignorant of my existence.

Having been at Magnus's shoulder throughout his life, I am alert to the reservations lurking at the back of his mind about a career as a marine engineer. I believe that with these misgivings Magnus's life on the ocean waves would be, at best, short lived.

****

For some young bloods, being an engineer at sea offered a marvellous future; an irresistible opportunity to maintain magnificent machinery, resolve complex mechanical and electrical problems or escape from the chilly drudgery of shipyard routine. For others it may appear a prison sentence, caged in the unbearably noisy, blisteringly hot and dangerous dungeon of an engine room. Crutch-enlivening prickly heat is one discomfort endured by many who venture into the sweat-box below decks. The daily dietary supplement of salt tablets, taken to fend-off stomach-churning fireman's cramp, may gift the seaman with hardening of the arteries and high blood pressure leading to face-hanging strokes later in life. These slow working poison pills, usually gulped down with gallons of Captain Cook's lime juice cure for scurvy, were to replace vital electrolytes and body fluids lost from being permanently drenched in sweat working below decks.

For Magnus, the adventure of travelling to faraway places was immensely exciting although, on closer inspection, some places with exotic names and risqué reputations proved to be less appealing than imagined. For instance, to find Bombay, it wasn't necessary to be guided by the ship's maps and compass or to rely upon the experience of a ship's pilot; from ten miles offshore, the quartermaster could steer the ship safely into port simply by following the stench from the city's fermented sewage discharge.

At sea, the engineering was practical, challenging and always interesting; unfortunately, the workplace was a hellhole. For Magnus, working in a ship's engine room was akin to going on a country drive while cooped up under the bonnet of the car with only an unbearably noisy engine for company. It was always greasy and sweaty-hot, seeing nothing and often unaware of whether it was day or night outside. Not an ideal existence for one who was at heart an outdoors-loving country boy.

When offered employment with Salvesen's, Magnus suppressed these misgivings in order to regain an occupation that offered a livelihood and potential security through continued education and employment.

With Salvesen's support, Magnus was to continue his studies at a marine college in Glasgow. He'd then ship out to the Southern Ocean for long stints embroiled in the wholesale slaughter of whales using barbed harpoons that exploded inside the giant creature's sleek and defenceless body. He had little appetite for this butchery, but had to earn a living; it was a choice between an unwholesome existence in the icy Antarctic seas or return to the dole queue until he secured other suitable employment.

His misgivings weren't confined to the hideous working conditions or living with the retching stench of putrid blubber which was reputed to be so cloyingly persistent that the rancid reek oozed from the whalers' pores for months after paying-off at the end of a voyage. Nor was it the horror of decks strewn with dismembered whale carcasses, or scuppers awash in a sloshing reservoir of icy blood; no, that wasn't the sum total of his apprehension. Late one night near the Hamburg docks, while still employed by Ellerman Lines, he'd witnessed the Scottish crew of a Salvesen's whaling ship at play, and the encounter had been chillingly impressive and mightily educational.

Magnus's ship, the pride of the fleet – the beautiful *City of Port Elizabeth* – aboard which he and other guest cadets had taken passage during their first Easter break from college, docked late at night in Hamburg. A small party, Magnus, another cadet and a couple of engineers, went shore-side for a nightcap at The Cabbage Patch, a notorious dockside haunt. Before reaching the pub it was obvious from the hullaballoo that a major battle was underway. Police cars with flashing lights were everywhere, and a contingent of giant German policemen, armed with skull-cracking nightsticks and dangerous looking handguns, stood about quietly waiting for the fracas to die down.

The railed-off courtyard surrounding The Cabbage Patch was a blur of red and black as a waterfall of scruffy tartan-clad buccaneer look-alikes poured through windows and doorways to continue their free-for-all with anybody who wasn't one of their own. Magnus learned that the clannish thugs were the white Scottish crew of a Salvesen ship who, like the whalers of old, were letting off steam after a prolonged period hunting and rendering down majestic whales in icy climes.

Even after repeatedly being turned away by the police, the electrical engineer in Magnus's party remained doggedly determined to brave the riot and enter The Cabbage Patch.

"No English or Scottish peoples in Patch tonight," ordered the goliath policeman guarding the entry gate.

"But there's somebody I must see," the electrician whined.

"No English! No Scottish men!" repeated the policeman with a calm, detached authority that brooked no challenge and suggested the mayhem was normal.

"Is Coca-Cola Hanna in tonight?" the electrician asked a buxom blond woman leaning against the courtyard side of the railing, away from the faltering mayhem.

"Coca-Cola not on game no more," the blond replied. "She go straight now. Work as clippie on Hamburg metro".

Not to let the night go unexplored, and adopting the sound nautical dictate of 'any port in a storm', the electrician propositioned the blond.

"No chance," she laughingly replied. "I on job-lot. I go to Scottish men's ship when they finish fun, smashing head."

Later, ejected from The Patch, well pleased with the night's entertainment, the shabby, battle-weary Scottish crew from the Leith-based whaler, shuffled past Magnus's group. Amongst the ragged rabble, one figure stood out – the blond working girl – ready to ply her trade until the early hours.

The randy electrician looked on, hardly able to contain his jealous irritation. In a final fling of frustration, he tried to charm any of the remaining women to service his needs, but without success. That night it seemed, 'No English! No Scottish!' applied not only to entering The Cabbage Patch, but also to the electrician's desire to sample any dockland delights.

Chapter 4 – The Engineer

****

Man is condemned to be free; because once thrown into the world,
He is responsible for everything he does.
Freedom is what you do with what's been done to you.

Jean-Paul Sartre (1905 – 1980)

****

To sea or not to sea, that was the dilemma. Around the time Salvesen's employment offer was made, Magnus's sister, Susan Maureen, who lived in England with her journalist husband, Alan, overheard pub-talk that a local company, Hawker Siddeley Aviation, was recruiting trainee engineers. Magnus made a prompt application and, much to his surprise and delight, was accepted as a trainee graduate engineer.

Salvesen's Marine Superintendent was mightily disgruntled on learning the news, but Magnus was not; after all he'd seen and smelled Salvesen's blood on the Hamburg docklands, and it wasn't commercial whale's blood at that, but the scarlet froth oozing from the flared nostrils and ripped lips of the company's battle-weary Scottish crew. He also had major reservations about sailing on white-crewed ships. He'd recently learned that a Manx friend who had gone to sea topside, as a Deck Officer Cadet, had suffered a fractured skull after being brutally beaten by sadistic members of his own ship's British crew.

Providence, destiny, or mere chance had again guided Magnus to the greener pastures of aviation and away from a seafarer's life toiling in the oppressive and claustrophobic engine rooms of merchant ships. For this unexpected opportunity he was flying high and undeniably grateful.

Hawker Siddeley Aviation was a massive enterprise specialising in the design and production of aeroplanes with factories throughout the British Isles and affiliates around the world. In due course Magnus was assigned to work at both Manchester factories. Structural components of planes, (fuselage, wings, tail-planes etc.) were formed and fabricated at the Chadderton factory. These components were transported across the city to be assembled and fitted out at the Woodford plant, from where the finished aircraft were delivered to the new owners.

Both factories dated back to World War II when aircraft production was frantic and Lancaster Bombers were being manufactured faster than the Luftwaffe and German anti-aircraft ground fire could blast them out of the sky. And bring down the bombers the enemy did. Of about 7,000 Lancaster Bombers built during that insane conflict, most were shot down with the loss of approximately 55,000 aircrew of Bomber Command.

Magnus started work with Hawker Siddeley in the autumn of 1964 when the HS 748 twin turbo-prop passenger plane and its military adaptation, the HS 780, were on the production lines. The HS 748 was designed as a replacement for the hundreds of ageing Douglas DC3 aircraft that had seen service around the world since before World War II, a quarter of a century earlier. Also, the pterodactyl-like Vulcan V-bomber and Shackleton Coastal Command aircraft (a modified version of the Lancaster Bomber) were continuously being refitted and upgraded in the Woodford hangers. The two factories combined catered for nearly every specialised aspect of forward-looking aircraft production, metallurgical and design engineering. For this reason, and the educational opportunities offered, Hawker Siddeley Aviation was an ideal corporation in which to be employed as a trainee graduate engineer.

Magnus's yearly activities were divided into two more-or-less equal modules of college study and applied factory work. He enjoyed the study, and by applying himself, became a diligent and successful student; however, the work periods in the factories were a different matter entirely. To a young blood with a yen for the freedom of outdoors, and who had sailed the seven seas before he was nineteen, the rigid discipline of clocking in and out of a factory amounted to a self-imposed prison term in an atmosphere that stifled the spirit and curtailed an individual's zest for life. Work on the factory production line was a sequence of dreary 'observation' assignments in an atmosphere where high-pitched screaming air drills tortured the brain and the suffocating smell of synthetic adhesives constricted the throat.

A very English class-driven surly obsequiousness, which most employees embraced as second nature, had inveigled itself into every aspect of factory life. The canteens, and even the lavatories, were segregated – apartheid fashion – into factory workers, weekly and monthly staff, and executive grades. Magnus's designated place in this hierarchical caste system for meals and bowel movements was amongst the weekly staff. He did however, venture into the factory workers' canteen on the occasion that the BBC was broadcasting its popular wireless programme, *Worker's Playtime*, from there. And once was enough. More mashed potatoes seemed to be thrown hither and yon than found its way into the factory workers' gullets.

The toilet facilities were equally stratified and ghettoised. Magnus found the secluded, two cubicle, monthly staff lavatories more comfortable and fresh than the weekly staff's line of whiffy flush toilet stalls or the windowless, bacterial breeding grounds that were the factory workers' running-trough coops.

Even considering these minor irritants, Magnus's time in aviation was happy, productive and provided a good foundation upon which to build a future career as a Chartered Engineer. It was an opportunity for which he always remained indebted. He'd made good friends and survived several serious romances there, but on moving away he lost touch. No matter how many New Year resolutions he made, Magnus remained a hopeless networker throughout his life.

Towards the end of his five years in aviation he made several attempts to gain employment that might be more agreeable than the robotic conformity of factory life. He was unsuccessful in an attempt to join BOAC as a trainee flight engineer (now an extinct species as their specialised services were replaced by control computers). He also failed to impress London-based OCL as a potential design engineer engaged in the containerisation of shipping.

The only job he was accepted for was as crew on a three masted schooner. The *Golden Cachalote*, formally a Baltic trader, was being refitted at Faversham in Kent as a charter vessel to carry passengers on naturalists' holidays around the Galapagos Islands in the Pacific Ocean – but more on this later.

In retrospect, Magnus's desire to leave aviation was perhaps rather short-sighted. Through hard work and application his examination successes rendered him eligible to attend Cranfield University to complete an Air Transport Management MSc with Hawker Siddeley acting as sponsor. However, this was not to be; his erratic, adventurous nature won the day.

During the late 1960's Magnus found two popular TV drama series to be essential viewing, and one of these programmes would have a profound influence upon his next direction of travel. *The Plane Makers* addressed the political chicanery and double dealing amongst the top echelons within the British aviation industry. He enjoyed the programme, but didn't need the series to understand that factory-based aircraft manufacture wasn't for him. The dramatic piece that truly captured his imagination and influenced his future was *The*

Troubleshooters. This series tackled exciting crises in the oil exploration industry and featured Australian actor Ray Barrett as the action man who travelled the world solving critical problems for a major oil company.

In the spring of 1969 a small classified advertisement in Britain's Daily Telegraph newspaper stated that a French company, GeoServices, was recruiting a variety of technical personnel to train as 'geologist' for work in the oil exploration industry.

What more could he ask for? This was a 'get out of factory-jail free' card. He attended an interview in New Bond Street, London, and was immediately offered a position. Although Magnus more than satisfied the job description criteria, his cultural heritage may have also worked in his favour. The interviewer was a Frenchman from Brittany and an influential member of the separatist Free Breton Movement. Brittany is a region in France with close historical and ethnic ties to the ancient Celtic tribes of the British Isles, from which the Manx bloodlines, due to their historic isolation, are directly descended.

Magnus thought it unwise to enlighten the Frenchman that, in his case, claims to a long Celtic heritage were only partially true. DNA mapping on his father's side had read 100% Norse Viking, sullied only slightly by the merest hint of Manx

Neanderthal blood. The slender Stone Age connection didn't surprise Magnus's brother, James Arthur Radcliffe. He knew perfectly well that Manx Neanderthals weren't an extinct species. On any Saturday afternoon in the Nursery Hotel's smoke-filled public bar there was a whole troop of them slouched in the back corner slugging pints and grunting excitedly at horse-racing broadcast live on TV.

Not surprisingly, after nearly five good years in Manchester, the draw of the familiar remained strong, but soon aviation and all that went with it were cast off. Magnus soon found his feet as a free agent forging a new future, and Paris provided the space and opportunities to do just that.

Three weeks after abandoning the monotonous routine of Hawker Siddeley factory life, and with only a taste of the geological training under his belt, Magnus found himself bouncing across the Algerian Sahara Desert in the back of a long-wheel-based Land Rover. The vehicle was jam-packed with robed and turban clad Arabs and desert dwelling Berbers. One of these nomads smiled a good deal to show off his tribal status with a full set of nicotine and betel nut stained gold-capped teeth. Crammed in the back of the truck, Magnus found viewing the passing barren scene nearly impossible, but he did get a close-up view of those gilded gnashes which were a ghastly sight indeed.

Occasionally the truck pulled over so passengers could stretch their legs, relieve themselves or crunch through a sandy chicken drumstick. After several hours they stopped at the foot of a desolate rock-strewn hill on the side of which was scattered a village of mud-rendered buildings. The travellers entered a roadside adobe through a bead curtain fly-screen into the cool darkness within. Once his eyes adjusted to the gloom, Magnus was both intrigued and amused at what he saw. They'd entered a cafe in which the customers weren't dusty shepherds as might have been expected, but a cluster of desert spivs, dressed in black and white striped double-breasted zoot-suits. Each wilderness wide-boy sported big, slicked-back, Elvis hair and shave-pointed sideburns. The new arrivals joined the suits to drink muddy coffee from miniature glass cups, before heading off ever southwards into the never-ending rock and sandy wasteland.

Their destination was an onshore oil exploration site near the Moroccan/Algerian border on latitude close to that of the Canary Islands, the same islands to which Magnus's grandfather had sailed to load cargos of bananas. At that time Algeria was undergoing major social upheaval as the political rivals, Boumediene and Ben Bella, had been vying for the country's top job after rejecting the French President's (Charles De Gaulle) ill-advised attempt at union between Algeria and France. The whole country seemed to be bristling with machine guns and camouflaged tanks on dusty manoeuvres.

After a dull and thankfully short job familiarisation stint amongst the rocky dunes of the Algerian Sahara, Magnus was recalled to Paris to complete training at inner city Place St George and suburban Clamart. His fellow trainees were a mixed bag of international hopefuls.

Several months later, he was assigned to work in Italy. He joined the American offshore oil rig *Spindletop*, named after the legendary salt dome oil field discovered in the 'Lone Star State' of Texas where, so Americans claim, the modern oil industry was born. The rig was a floating platform constructed around the hull of a sea-going barge originally designed to transport railroad stock between the lower 48 States of the USA and Alaska. The oil exploration industry working the Italian sector of the Adriatic Sea was based in the delightful ship building seaport of Ancona, which became Magnus's shore-side base.

The work roster was two weeks of daily twelve hour shifts aboard *Spindletop*, followed by a week shore-side in Ancona. During one of these weeks ashore he jumped an overnight ferry to

Zadar, a seaport since before Roman times on the Yugoslavian Dalmatian Coast. On arrival, a tourist information officer directed him to a house that offered bed and breakfast. With no forward booking, and the locals keen to make a quid, he was thankful to accept the only remaining space in town – a bed-settee in the household's lounge.

At the beach, Magnus must have seemed a feeble translucent apparition against the healthy looking, sun-bronzed locals cavorting freely in the sparkling azure sea. He was a skinny snow white organism with bright blue eyes and a shock of red hair, only able to wallow at the water's edge because he was unable to swim a single stroke.

After a day exploring, and an evening dining on the local speciality, chevapchichi, washed down with a carafe of the regional red wine, he was contented, hang-dog tired and ready for bed. However, it wasn't to be. Back at his digs, on opening the lounge door to his makeshift bedroom, he was confronted by the entire household and what he took to be members of their extended family, sitting on and about his bed-settee watching television. Magnus spoke neither Croat nor Italian nor Russian nor German, and none of the tonne and a half of humanity hogging his bed spoke English, so communication was somewhat fraught. He was rather put-out at having his bedroom invaded, but when they happily offered him a chair and a glass of local spirit, slivovitz, what could he do but sit down and join the party. What they were watching on the black and white TV had him baffled. All that could be seen were vague shadows milling about like slow motion deep-sea divers fully kitted-out in underwater regalia with pressure helmets, air tanks and weighted boots. The drink flowed, the party proceeded and he waited patiently for the Croat mob hogging his bed-settee to leave so he could spirit-up a little much-needed dreamtime.

Several glasses of hooch later he realised that he wasn't watching a murky underwater adventure of Lloyd Bridges' Sea Hunt on a faulty TV. What his bedroom-squatters were toasting and cheering so heartily, along with 600 million TV viewers worldwide, was none other than the live broadcast of the first manned landing and human footprint on the moon made by Neil Armstrong, an American astronaut. Throughout the entire spectacle, their behaviour was closely monitored under the steely gaze of Yugoslavia's benevolent dictator, Marshal Tito, whose twice life-sized framed and glazed likeness peered down on them from a vantage point high on the lounge room wall.

Occasionally wild storms from the Russian Steppes surged southwards through Eastern Europe throwing up mountainous waves across the normally benign Adriatic Sea, creating danger to shipping. One such tempest proved too lively for the flat-bottomed *Spindletop* and all non-essential personnel were forced to abandon ship. They were rescued and taken aboard a Norwegian, Ned Lloyd, rig supply boat. The leap from *Spindletop*'s unnaturally lurching deck onto the thrashing deck of the rescue boat, pitching and corkscrewing alongside, proved to be a hair-raising escapade. The iron grip on Magnus's arm by a tree trunk sized Norwegian deckhand was the necessary confidence booster to make the move.

Aboard the rescue boat as it rolled, bucked and heaved towards the port of Ancona, most of the Italians – oil workers, catering staff and drilling superintendents – cowered foetal-like in bunks or rolled helplessly back and forth across the passenger cabin deck amidst a slop of oily, tomato-laced vomit. The acrid puke caked their clothes, hair and faces with threads of half-digested spaghetti and blotchy red Bolognese sauce. Magnus had never seen any group of people so dispirited, all hope gone, seemingly awaiting the blessed relief of death. Meanwhile, to escape the pathetic groaning and stench of vomit, Magnus spent most of the trip topside or on the bridge, exhilarated by the mighty seas and soaring deck, with which he was familiar.

During the roller-coaster ride to their home port, whilst the rescue vessel was tossed on to the crest of a mountainous wave, Magnus was astonished to glimpse a submarine's periscope break the surface in the trough between two mighty waves not thirty metres off their port beam. It's interesting to speculate which of the two vessels would have fared worst, had the Ned Lloyd rescue boat surfed down the back side of a wave to crash, with catastrophic force, into the hapless submarine below.

Instability in the heavy seas was the death knell for the *Spindletop*. She was towed into Ancona where she remained lashed to the quay-side, awaiting a new drilling contract in calmer waters.

In need of a new assignment, Magnus was sent to the gigantic Italian semi-submersible rig, *Scarabeo*. His first encounter with this 20-storey monster wasn't disembarking from a crew relief helicopter in the sunlit daytime hours, but hoist aboard by crane from the heaving deck of a rig service vessel in the dead of night. The hair-raising ride from the midnight blackness of the boat onto the floodlit rig high above, whilst standing on a tiny wooden platform and white-knuckle gripping a thick rope net attached to a crane hook, was a terrifying experience. When dangling fifty metres above the oil-black sea, the crane driver may spice-up the occasion by jolting the hoist-line as a friendly 'welcome aboard' gesture. Now that's a surprise greeting guaranteed to drain the blood from the face of all but the most unimaginative.

Magnus lived aboard two further rigs during the seven months working in the Adriatic, the French drillship *Neptune Gascoigne*, and an ancient Italian jack-up rust-bucket, the name of which he's long forgotten.

It was waiter service and linen serviettes in the dining saloons aboard the three European registered and manned rigs, with wine and beer as you wished. The American rig was quite the contrary – a military style 'line up and help yourself' mess that was dry as a bone. For all their crowing of constitutional freedom, there appeared to remain a solid lobby for containment and prohibition amongst the influential political classes in Washington DC. These so-called elites appear to cling to the conviction that their own countrymen are unable to act responsibly in their own or others' best interests when it comes to the consumption of alcohol. And, judging from Magnus's experience of some American oil workers at play shore-side, they may well be right.

Without doubt, the European rigs were the most comfortable on which to live and work, but the Italian helicopter service left a lot to be desired. They were deadly. During his seven months in Italian waters, three helicopters servicing the rigs on which he'd worked mysteriously crashed into the sea leaving no survivors.

A stylish and charming Italian colleague, Bertolli, whose priorities in life were fast cars, good food and beautiful women – in no particular order, just so long as they were plentiful and available – died in one of these disasters. It was assumed the pilot of the low-flying helicopter lost track of the horizon when altering course towards the coast in a thick dawn fog and flew directly into the sea at over 160 kilometres per hour, killing all aboard.

During his time on the Adriatic, Magnus picked up enough Italian to do his job with an efficient, albeit humorous, way of communicating with the rig personnel. Part of his job was to alert them of drilling breaks or the presence of combustible or poisonous gas. Normal conversation was, however, a dead loss so he requested a transfer. The Paris head office graciously obliged, offering a choice between Abu Dhabi and Australia. In the late 1960's Abu Dhabi wasn't the air-conditioned tourist paradise it is today. At that time, it was a traditional Persian Gulf trading port, unbearably hot and with near 100 per cent humidity – not a desirable place to be unless possessed of the disposition of Lawrence of Arabia.

During his sea-time in the merchant navy, Magnus had spent nearly two months partying and loading cargo at all the major Australian ports and had greatly liked what he'd seen. So once again he was Australia bound.

Chapter 5– The geologist

****

I've done made a deal with the devil.
He said he's going to give me an air-conditioned place,
if I go there, so I won't put all the fires out.

Paul Neal (Red) Adair (1915 – 2004)

Oil well fire fighter (Well Killer)

****

The flight to Australia seemed never-ending. The Boeing 707 put down and took off a mind-numbing eighteen times. Bartering for a 24-carat gold five-piece interlaced ring puzzle whilst half asleep in the bazaar-like Beirut airport was a mild but temporary distraction. The only excitement during the flight was aborting the Hong Kong landing as the wheels were about to meet the seawater-bounded runway. At the best of times, landing at Hong Kong airport was a heart-in-the-mouth experience as the airliner appeared to be flying between the taller city buildings before touching down. The 707's engines roared into life, the plane was thrown into a steep climb, and mountain tops whizzed past the portholes. Why the landing was aborted, the passengers never discovered; the only announcement was the diversion to The Philippines.

All aboard were accommodated overnight in a luxury marble and crystal chandelier Manila hotel whilst the aircraft flew back to Hong Kong to collect the stranded passengers. Magnus was allocated an enormous suite of rooms, one of which housed a bed as big as a normal sized bedroom. Had the Paris office paid an advance before the flight Down Under, he could easily have succumbed to some of the special room service 'delights' on offer. The house specialties included The Relaxer, The Royal Treatment, and The Emperor's Delights. Perhaps, for once, having no money was a saving grace.

His employer's Australian office was located in Brisbane, where he teamed-up with a familiar face from training in Paris. Mike arrived from Churchill, the polar bear tourist paradise on Hudson Bay, in Quebec province, north eastern Canada. Quite a shock to the system for Mike – one day in the super-chilled Arctic winter at twenty degrees below, the next in the hot and humid sub-tropical Queensland summer at thirty above.

"Hello Mike," Magnus said. "Is that sunburn or chilblains you're sporting on your cheeks?"

"G'day Blue," replied the gnome-like Mike, grinning widely, "nothing of the kind, just an exxy Arctic tan."

If nothing else, Mike was adaptable; he'd been in Australia for only one day and already was at home with the local vernacular.

The pair was assigned to an American deep water semi-submersible rig, the SEDCO 135G. Their new home was located in the Timor Sea, about an hour by chopper off Darwin, the capital of Australia's 'wild west' frontier, the Northern Territory. They arrived at The Top End – as it's affectionately known amongst the locals – at the end of January 1970. Fortunately, they'd missed the tropical 'suicide season' by a month or more, but still arrived during The Wet when the stiflingly hot and nearly 100% humid air is difficult to breathe.

The rig was required to drill a relief well to choke-off and plug a gas blowout. Some months earlier, whilst drilling at a depth of about 11,000ft, a high pressure gas reservoir was discovered. Over several hours, the drill crew lost control of the well, allowing a gas surge to explode and creating an intense fire storm, 100 metres high. Surprisingly nobody was killed, but the rig was badly damaged and had to be towed to Singapore for repair.

For the following 16 months, gas continued to surge and burn on the water's surface. Flames licked 20 metres into the air, burning bright yellow above an acre or so of the gas-cut sea. The spectacular inferno was only visible after dark; during daylight the boiling ocean surface was the only evidence that gas was escaping.

Occasionally Mother Nature played games at the oilmen's expense; she snuffed out the blaze with a combined assault from high seas, cyclonic winds and torrential monsoonal rain. During daylight hours, the escaping gas presented only a limited danger to shipping as the turbulent and bubbling sea was clearly visible and easily avoided. At night the blazing gas was a glowing beacon that could be seen from 20 miles away. Only the insane, or perhaps a Russian flagged freighter, would knowingly approach the inferno. When the gas was not burning, a passing ship, venturing too close to the rig during the hours of darkness could sail into the gas-cut sea, lose buoyancy, and sink 600 feet to the seabed.

Re-igniting the leaking gas necessitated some head scratching and several eccentric solutions were proposed and tried. John Lenin and Yoko Ono put great store in the exercise of imagination, but it's doubtful that they could have dreamt up solutions as improbable and hare-brained as did the rig's tool pushers. A large drum, filled with blazing waste, was slung on a wire attached to the rig and to a service vessel stationed beyond the gas-cut sea, about 500 metres from the rig. The flames burned through the drum's attachment before it had run 20 metres along the wire, sending the flaming container plummeting into the sea. Unlike the success enjoyed by Francis Drake when his fire ships singed the King of Spain's beard in 1587, floating a raft of flaming oil drums into the gas cloud was the second failure; the raft sank, dousing the blazing contents. An American tool pusher nicknamed Shoot (Shoot the Son of a Bitch), because of his bow and arrow hunting obsession when ashore on leave, attempted the Geronimo method of fire lighting. He struck the Apache warrior's stance and loosed flaming arrows from the deck of a service vessel into the gas cloud. This highly theatrical redskin lookalike's performance fared no better than the flaming drum-in-the-drink fiasco. Ultimately however, a successful process was discovered. A ship's distress flare was fired into the gas which ignited with an almighty whoosh that may well have singed the eyebrows off the brave soul who squeezed the signal gun's trigger.

The new arrivals in Darwin, Magnus and Mike, together with various associated oil exploration personnel, were billeted at the Fanny

Bay Hotel. This splendid seaside building, together with most of the township of Darwin, was trashed by cyclone Tracey on Christmas Eve four years later. While the two strangers in town limbered up with pre-dinner drinks, they were approached by a very grim looking geologist from Aquitaine, the French oil company and the organisation for which they were contracted to work.

"The rig service boat, *SEDCO Helen*, has sunk and nine of her crew are missing," the Frenchman informed them. "Merde! Catastrophique! She sank in minutes, while laying down positioning anchors for our rig."

It seemed a bulky retrieval buoy had become snagged in a marker line and was yanked deep underwater by a plunging ten tonne anchor. On breaking free from the entanglement, the buoy's buoyancy sent the heavy steel float rocketing to the surface with mighty force. Unfortunately, it didn't surge out of the sea like a leaping whale, but smashed into the vessel's hull, ripping off a steel stern plate and leaving a gaping hole, which allowed seawater to flood the engine room and down went the *SEDCO Helen* together with nine of her crew to the seabed, 600 feet below.

An alternative service vessel was found, the disaster being no more than a tragic and expensive industrial statistic. Magnus lived under no delusions about his own importance. If he was injured or killed on the rig; he'd be flown ashore, immediately replaced, and just as quickly forgotten.

A French colleague did experience a life changing accident on another offshore rig. The wire which feeds an instrument to measure the rate of drilling and depth of the hole had jumped off its jockey-pulley. The Frenchman wrapped the wire around his hand in the hope of flicking it back onto the pulley. Unfortunately, at that moment, the driller dropped the travelling block, to which the wire was attached, heaving the Frenchman 30 feet into the air. The wire snatched, severing his hand across the palm, releasing him to fall onto the rig's steel deck smashing his face and teeth and crippling his other hand. These dreadful injuries rendered him unemployable, and within a year or two his family life was torn apart in the divorce courts.

As ever, industry marched on regardless of events – make hole, make hole, make hole – that's the mantra and all that counts in the oil patch, apart from making fat profits.

Magnus worked aboard the *SEDCO 135G* for eleven months during which time no more lives were lost, although several fingers were crushed or nipped off between rolling drill pipes.

By November, as progress on the relief well neared the final stage of communication with the blowout zone, the rig became critically overcrowded with all manner of oil field blowout specialists, including Coots (Well Killer) Matthews, a senior member of the legendary Red Adair stable.

During the final well-plugging operation, the whole rig shuddered and rattled to the roar of a dozen or more giant diesel and gas turbine mud pumps which were temporarily rigged-up on the main deck. The pumps were employed to stifle the blowout, initially with sea water, followed by heavy drilling mud, and finally the escaping gas was sealed off by pumping quick-setting cement into the well.

The pumps were run full-bore until they seized or blew up, when they were immediately replaced. Amidst this cacophonous racket and billowing clouds of choking exhaust fumes, it wasn't only "Cough-a-Lot" Sims, a chain-smoking tool pusher who suffered; all aboard the rig endured interrupted sleep, sore throats, inflamed eyes and running noses. It wasn't a healthy or comfortable place to be.

On shore leave, not long after arriving in Darwin, Magnus attended one of the celebrated 'Late Nights' in the Darwin Hotel which had the only air conditioned cocktail bar in town. There he met the mascara-eyed, choker-wearing, adventurous blond, Sophia Elizabeth, who was exploring her homeland with two friends. A fortunate meeting for him as it was her first night in town allowing her insufficient time to get attached to some other lucky soul. For the remainder of their time in the Northern Territory, Sophia and Magnus became wonderfully close, spending most of their time together when he was ashore.

Around the time Sophia returned home to Brisbane where her newly graduated brother was to be married, the gas blowout was choked off and consequently Magnus was released from rig duties. With the relief well completed, he was to be transferred to Asia, but first returned to Brisbane for revaccination against yellow fever, cholera and typhoid. On the long flight from Darwin he teamed up with a rig colleague from the Australian Government's Bureau of Mineral Resources and together they enjoyed a splendid time swigging Gordon's gin and reminiscing about the past year's goings-on aboard the 135G and other oil patch gossip.

Sophia and her brother Robert collected Magnus from the Brisbane airport, for he'd been invited to stay at their parents' home. He was full of gin and good humour and Sophia was happy to see him, but an oddly subdued atmosphere pervaded in the car. This unsettling mood of mild gloominess continued at their home. Magnus failed to grasp the significance of a large stack of gift-wrapped packages in the middle of the lounge carpet. However, it soon became apparent what bombshell had stunned the household.

Robert was to have been married that very day, but had prevaricated, taking his second thoughts right up to the wire. He'd called off the wedding just twenty-four hours before the fateful words "I do" were scheduled to float between the loving couple. Understandably, everybody except Magnus felt somewhat deflated at missing a good day out. However, the household soon discovered how a healthy dose of high-altitude gin could help break the ice to let in a chink of cheer. Over the next few days the household returned to happy normality, and Magnus was made most welcome, feeling quite at home before heading off to exotic Asia.

His new assignment was aboard an American drillship located in the South China Sea; not far off the coast of Vietnam. At that time, the war between the Americans and Ho Chi Minh's Viet Cong was raging, and occasionally an American military aircraft would fly low to buzz the rig.

Magnus's accommodation aboard the rig was appalling, a minuscule two-berth cabin where he and his co-worker were expected to hot-bed with members of the Indonesian crew. On the other hand, the American drilling personnel and Italian oil company representatives lived in spacious two-berth cabins with only a single occupant. Since arriving on the rig, Magnus had had a running battle with the Barge Master who was responsible for allocating rig-board living accommodation. This bigoted Yankee imbecile was a coarse tobacco-chewing hillbilly whose only claim to fame was that the blood in his veins was reputed to be one-sixteenth Cherokee. What this mongrel's remaining blood supply was made-up of was anybody's guess; Magnus supposed creosote the most probable. Magnus persistently lobbied and cajoled the spineless Italians, who hired the rig and for whom he was contracted to work, to provide suitable accommodation for himself and his colleague. Eventually they were allocated bunks in the ship's hospital, an improvement, but only just.

In general, Magnus had enjoyed working with Americans from a wide cross section of society and from various States of the Union. Some of the American personnel working on the rig in the South China Sea were however, a different breed entirely. They were the most unpleasant men he'd had to endure during the entire time he worked in oil exploration. Whoever recruited these degenerates seemed to have gone out of their way to scour the xenophobic dregs from a cesspit of American oilfield rejects.

But it wasn't all misery. The shore-side base was Singapore, and even though in the early 1970's the island state still gave off a lingering whiff of bad drains, it remained a mysterious and exotic place to reconnoitre. The recent riotous behaviour of

American GI's on Rest and Recuperation leave from war-torn Vietnam had ceased and Singapore had regained its poise and dignity again. In the over-crowded island city state, all the oriental delights of wine, women and song were still available and in never-ending supply, but Magnus's heart lay elsewhere.

Throughout this period, Magnus and Sophia maintained a regular flow of airmail correspondence. At the time, there were no internet and international landline telephone calls were expensive and rarely used. After a big cognac-swigging night celebrating his Chinese hotel owner's first grandson's first month of life, Magnus's thoughts, as they often did, turned to Sophia. To hear her soft comforting voice, he took the unusual step of phoning her in Brisbane. Unfortunately, he'd got the time difference between Singapore and eastern Australia the wrong way round, so Sophia's phone rang while the household was fast asleep. Alarmed at the possibility of an emergency (for why else would anybody call in the middle of the night), Sophia's parents hurriedly called her to the phone. On hearing her dreamy voice Magnus realised how much he missed her and commented on how happy he was to hear her soft Aussie burr. In his state of late night woozy euphoria, he cooed these slurred endearments repeatedly.

During the remainder of his leave in Singapore he composed a letter in which he speculated on the idea of marriage. Back on the rig, where receiving letters was a greatly anticipated luxury, he eagerly awaited a reply.

Sophia's letter duly arrived, but it wasn't what he'd hoped for. He got a flea-in-the-ear for waking and upsetting the whole household in the middle of the night and repeatedly harping-on about her accent, which she took as an insult to her proud Australian heritage.

Naturally Magnus was nonplussed and flabbergasted on reading the letter, and agonised over what to do. He finally elected to do nothing for a few days, as the timing suggested that letters must have crossed in the post. After a week of anxious anticipation, a second letter arrived and the contents were much more to his liking. An interchange of airmail sealed their fate and Sophia would make all arrangements for the wedding to take place in Brisbane some two months later.

Once again, like so many things in his life, all he had to do was be there. And therein lay a seemingly insurmountable problem.

Inconveniently, the Singapore manager had gone on an extended vacation to Europe and Magnus's rig relief had been appointed as the temporary company representative in the Singapore office for the duration of the manager's absence.

These arrangements prevented Magnus leaving the rig, let alone making wedding and travel plans. He remained trapped in the middle of the South China Sea and, with every passing week, the wedding day was edging closer. After two months of protest and threats, he finally learnt that his prolonged incarceration aboard the unhappy drillship was about to end. His colleague would return with the next crew change and Magnus would be able to climb aboard the Bristow helicopter en route for the volcanic island of Natuna Besar where the crew handovers took place.

"Iffa your relief is notta on the plane, pleasea makea sure you comea back," pleaded Macanyani, the Italian geologist. "Pleasea Magnus, it is a très importante."

This was the proviso attached to his release. If his relief wasn't aboard the plane from Singapore, he had to return to the rig. Oil exploration requires a full complement of hands to ensure round the clock work continues uninterrupted.

The Douglas DC3 touched down on the rough grass strip situated between the base of an enormous volcano and a picturesque lagoon infested with sea snakes and sharks. Magnus studied those disembarking from the antique plane with a mixture of annoyance and apprehension. If his relief didn't appear, what would he do? Abandon his responsibilities and climb aboard the plane to journey to his future bride, or return to work aboard an unhappy drillship vibrating with hate and tribal tensions? If he returned to the rig, Sophia's family would suffer their second wedding cancellation within six months and, in all probability, he'd have to look elsewhere for nuptial happiness.

One of the last to disembark the plane was the short fat Luxembourgian he'd hoped to see. Magnus didn't greet his colleague with word or gesture, just followed him with his eyes in a face that radiated contempt and loathing for leaving him trapped on the rig for so long. The Luxembourgian wasn't entirely detestable though; he'd cultivated a zany streak that on occasions reflected a whimsical Dadaist humour. He had once boasted in a thickly accented outburst: "If I am very rich, I replace millions of otel Gideon Bibles wiss look-a-likes which when opened, go bang and fire electric shock up ze arms of nosey parker."

The newly arrived relief crew boarded the Bristow helicopter and flew onward to the drillship leaving the grass airstrip clear. The Indonesians going to Tanjung Pinang and the Westerners bound for Singapore clambered aboard the old DC3 that had just flown in, and belted-up ready for take-off.

The aeroplane engines throbbed, the propellers whined and the aircraft bounced alarmingly until the brakes were let go. In an instant the plane bounded and skipped along the rough grass airstrip rapidly gathering speed. With an almighty explosion, the starboard propeller stopped dead, the plane slewed violently sideways, and smoking oil spewed out of the right-hand engine vents across the wing. The plane lurched to a standstill, and with the other engine smothered, all was white-faced stillness and silence. Once those aboard realised they weren't going to be catapulted into the lagoon and death had been deferred for another day, they spilled onto the airstrip as fast as they could escape, cheerfully slapping one another on the back, laughing and hooting madly as they went.

So there they were, with a broken aeroplane, somewhere in the South China Sea, trapped on a narrow strip of land on the coastal flank of a monstrous volcano.

"Now what?" Magnus mused. "At last a dash for freedom, and now this."

However, things are rarely as bad as they seem. The helicopter base was designed with emergency situations in mind and had ample dining and sleeping accommodation for all. Also, a different crew from another oil rig was to be relieved the following day and there appeared to be two vacant seats on the flight to Singapore. As soon as Magnus heard this news, he started lobbying to secure one of the spare seats. It wasn't an easy task as he was up against tool pushers and drilling superintendents – Americans of influence who generally got their own way – the very cohort who had denied him suitable living conditions on the drillship.

"I demand a seat on that plane. I've been trapped for eight weeks on that junk-heap in the middle of the South China Sea, and thanks to you lot, living in shithouse accommodation. Whilst during this time, you've enjoyed three stints of shore-side leave with your feet up swigging whiskey sours in the Raffles Long Bar. Also I'm not coming back. I've got nothing to lose, except missing my wedding in Australia, and I'm not doing that. I don't have second thoughts," he crowed through tight lips and with the bulging eyes of someone gone *troppo* from too long offshore.

Much to his surprise he got his way, but not before repeating similar threats and demands to all who could hear. It's unlikely that he endeared himself to anybody that day, nor made any new friends. The next morning, he was first to climb aboard the other DC3 to claim one of the two spare seats. However, he believed his case was just, and after the vile treatment from the Yankee Barge Master, a hint of pay back was sweet indeed. The loathsome sixteenth-part Cherokee redneck was one of those left behind; marooned on the volcanic island.

Three days later, dressed smartly in a dark blue suit and matching tie, Magnus relaxed in the Brisbane airport bar waiting to be collected after his flight from Singapore. His eyes caught a quick movement from behind his newspaper; he looked up to glimpse an exquisitely graceful form bounding in to the lounge. This leggy apparition of glowing good health and loveliness – sheathed in a figure-flattering, long-sleeved top, tantalising hot pants and stylish raised heel slippers, all in eye-catching scarlet – whose blond hair shone like silk against a matching scarlet beret, was beauty indeed.

"I came as fast as I could," gasped Sophia Elizabeth breathlessly. "Welcome home."

"Good gracious" Magnus thought. "This exquisite vision is here for me!"

For a moment he couldn't say anything – he just smiled in wonderment.

"You look gorgeous," was all he could manage; but thought, "You lucky dog Magnus."

And this fortuitous sequence of events was how the 27-year-old Magnus Henry came to call Australia home. And how eventually, Magnus and Sophia's daughters (Willow Victoria and Fenella Jeanette) and their five grandchildren learned to sing *Waltzing Matilda* as happy and contented 'True Blue'   Aussies.

Part 2

****

A VOLATILE VOYAGE THROUGH RETIREMENT

****

Chapter 6 – The Photographer

****

Take Dada seriously!
It's worth it.

George Grosz (1893 – 1959)

First Dada Festival, Berlin 1920

****

A powerful nostalgia may overtake emigrants living a great distance from where they were brought up, a sort of 'fantasised reminiscence'. An old Greek who migrated to Fremantle in Western Australia suffered from this wavering of place. When in Fremantle he'd often romanticise about his youth.

"In Greece I'd roam the mountain tops where the air was so heavy with the spicy oils of rosemary and thyme it made me soar, just like an angel to heaven."

He'd save money for a holiday back to Greece and, while there, playing backgammon with old friends in the village square café, he'd brag, "In Australia we have sardines this big!" holding his hands apart to show the fish's size, which was always bigger than the one that got away.

Magnus was sympathetic to the old Greek's dilemma of divided allegiance. For many years he kept one foot on the Isle of Man and the other foot in Australia. Ultimately, home was definitely Down Under, but his sentimental homeland remained the Isle of Man which he visited nearly annually.

The Isle of Man is mainly agricultural land – arable farmland and high-country sheep grazing. Being a small hilly island, with the sea never far away, it's laughingly said to have no climate, just weather. For somebody usually living in hot and humid Australia, the cooler northern hemisphere island is a perfect place for walking, and that's what Magnus did nearly every day on his trips back to the Isle of Man.

While exploring the countryside close to his mother's home, he'd often see a particular farmer inspecting livestock and crops, or trundling across fields on a mud-spattered tractor. Everything about the farmer's appearance was straight out of a 1930's handbook for 'stylish' Manx farmers. The grubby flat cap, patched tweed jacket, old corduroy strides tied with bailing twine around the ankles in case a startled rat made a dash for safety up his trouser leg, a frayed flannelette shirt under an ancient waistcoat that may have once belonged to his grandfather, and on his feet, a pair of stout black hobnailed boots. Whenever the farmer was to be seen, there too was his sheepdog, a keenly attentive Border Collie.

If Magnus caught the farmer's eye, he'd give him a raised arm *sieg heil* style wave, and was pleased to receive a slowly raised hand of recognition in response or, if close-by, a light "Hey Boy" may waft through the air.

During one of his frequent visits to the island, Magnus came face to face with Willie Leece, although he never knew his name until years later on reading the farmer's obituary in the local newspaper:

****

Tribute to Willie Leece

Best Friends: Willie Leece and his constant companion, his dog, Gyp, both died on the same day at Ballaoates, St Johns.

Willie Leece died in the farm house he was born in 69 years ago and lived in all his life.

Following on from a well-known farming family he and his brother, Joe, farmed Ballaoates at St Johns, with Willie looking after the breeding and welfare of the livestock.

In his youth he was a member and chairman of the Central Young Farmers Club and went on to support events and farming organisations. "He had the great gift of being content with his life as a farmer. His neighbours respected him and will miss him greatly," said the Methodist Minister, the Reverend Grace Easthope, conducting his funeral service in St John's Methodist Chapel.

She told the congregation that in the afternoon of Willie's death his faithful dog, Gyp, died, too. "They will be reunited in heaven," she said.

Harvey Briggs
Isle of Man Examiner
Tuesday, 17 July, 2007

****

Early one bright spring morning Magnus met Willie on the narrow, twisty Ballaoates Road. Willie and his companion, the sheepdog Gyp, plodded uphill; Magnus, with gravity on his side, was making easy going of it trudging downhill.

"Hiya," he greeted Willie with a wave.

"Hello Yessir," Willie replied quietly. "At last I've put a sight on ya. Are ya local?"

"Originally I'm from Onchan, but now live in Australia," he replied. "At the moment I'm staying with my mother at The Hope".

"Australia's a long way away Boy," stated Willie looking into the distance. "What in heaven's name took you all that way from home?"

"Work," Magnus answered. "I used to work on oil rigs and was sent to Australia, and I've been there ever since. If we'd had a family farm though, I'd probably have done what you're doing and never left the island."

They talked in easy comfort for a while, and when Magnus felt it wouldn't be too intrusive, asked if he could take Willie's photograph.

"Oh, I don't know about that Yessir," he replied bashfully. "Who'd want a photo of me?"

Well Magnus did, and even though the pose wasn't exactly what he'd hoped for, he took a couple of shots. When he stood back to snap the pictures, Willie lifted Gyp so the dog was standing on its hind legs in front of him, whilst he looked down smiling shyly in mild embarrassment. It was an awkward pose, but it captured their togetherness.

"Do you take many snaps Yessir?" Willie asked quietly.

"Yes I do," Magnus replied. "And I'm particularly interested in the hedge sculptures and bailing twine creations along this road. Do you know anything about them?"

"You mean the hub caps and paint drums, and them sorts of things?" Willie asked.

"Yes. They're very unusual and whenever I'm on the island I make a point of walking through Archallagen to see what new works have appeared, and if there are any, I photograph them."

"Oh, I've been doin them for years," the farmer said hesitantly. "They're just bits and pieces from the farm and things I find on the road. Do you like them then Yessir?" he added bashfully.

"Very much," Magnus replied encouragingly, adding. "Do you mind if I take photographs in the fields and on the hedges?"

"Take as many photos as you like Boy," the farmer answered smiling. "And go in any of the fields you like."

Over the years, Magnus recorded hundreds of Willie's works in the hope of arranging an exhibition of the creations. In readiness for a showing, he'd already mounted and framed fifty or so enlarged photographs of Willie's more intriguing handiwork.

Around Easter 2013 Magnus approached the Sayle Gallery to enquire if they were interested in showing photographs of Willie's work. The gallery, in association with the Isle of Man Arts Council, specialised in promoting local arts and crafts, and frequently held exhibitions in the island's foremost display space on Douglas Promenade.

"Of course we're interested. These works are exactly the sort of local novelty we should be promoting," the gallery attendant stated enthusiastically. "Are you prepared to leave these sample photographs for appraisal by the exhibition selection committee?"

"Certainly," Magnus replied, delighted by the unexpectedly positive response. "There are plenty more framed and ready for hanging if needed."

For several months nothing was heard. Whenever he viewed a new exhibition at the gallery, he'd ask about the prospects for a Willie Leece showing. Encouraging noises were plentiful, but no commitment was forthcoming. Eventually, feeling he was getting the run-around, and that the gallery had lost interest in Willie's work, he'd more or less given up on the prospect of holding an exhibition.

Later that year, on a warm, good-to-be-alive September afternoon, he walked along Douglas promenade to meet his sister, Susan Maureen, arriving on the Liverpool ferry. Susan loved sea voyages, even if for only a few hours. Her spirits were high; her hair was enlivened by fresh gusts of salty air; and she was game for a stroll along the promenade.

"Do you fancy seeing the war artist's 'Response to Place' exhibition?" he proposed.

"Very much," she enthused.

Magnus had read about the block-buster Kurt Schwitters exhibition which had recently opened at the Sayle Gallery, following a successful season in London's Tate Britain art museum. He was aware of the World War II European internees and prisoners of war held on the island from attending earlier exhibitions at the Manx Museum, but had little knowledge of the specific artists amongst their number.

Susan Maureen had lectured in art history and appreciation for several years and was always keen to use her lively critical eye. Over the years, she and Magnus had attended several specialist exhibitions together, including the 2013 Royal Academy Summer Show in London.

"Has any decision been made about the Willie Leece photographs?" Magnus enquired of the gallery manager.

The manager turned to look at him with a distracted expression of perplexity written across his face. Strangely intrigued, he gazed for a moment before his vacant eyes opened wide into a wild stare and his jaw dropped in a flood of recognition.

"It's you," he spluttered, throwing his arms in the air in a crucifixion-like gesture of disbelief. "We've been going mad trying to find you. Our records are at fault and we had no way to contact you. Thank God it's you!" he continued, his Latvian accent more pronounced than usual.

"Well here I am," Magnus replied with surprised amusement. "What's the problem? Is Willie a goer or not?"

"We want your photographs as local interest for the Schwitters exhibition," the manager exclaimed with relief beaming across his face.

Now it was Magnus's turn to be thrown off balance; nothing had happened for months, and then suddenly it was nearly too late to be involved.

"They're framed and ready to hang," he said excitedly. "How many do you want and when do you want them?"

"All of them – and now," the manager replied cheerfully.

Magnus and Susan jumped into a taxi, loaded the framed photographs and delivered them to their fate; and that's how Willie Leece, the Manx agricultural abstractionist, became the support artist for the much anticipated Kurt Schwitters exhibition on the Isle of Man in the autumn of 2013.

The tenuous link between Willie Leece, a quiet Manx farmer, and the German born Kurt Schwitters, a giant of twentieth century art – wittily acknowledged by the vigilant curators of the Sayle Gallery exhibition – was the common creative impulse that oxygenated their psyches in a similar and often quirky fashion. Both artists worked with found materials, Willie Leece almost exclusively;

not so for Schwitters – his collage work was only a single facet of his treasure trove of artistic works.

The Manx exhibition of Schwitters art works was akin to a home-coming. Most of the works on display were created during his internment on the Isle of Man during World War II, as a reluctant guest of King George VI.

In 1930's Nazi Germany, Schwitters and his innovative ilk were branded as *Degenerate Artists*. It was the Fuhrer's *diktat* that this seditious group's anarchistic take on life flouted the Teutonic order of things, instead of exalting the *blood of the soil* values of racial purity, which was the official Nazi Party line. On seeing his paintings hung upside-down at the infamous 1937 Nazi Exhibition of Degenerate Art in Munich, Schwitters recognised the insult, but more importantly got the message, and fled to his beloved Norway to avoid Gestapo persecution or worse. The Norwegians must have taken Schwitters to heart because later, when the Nazi war machine rolled over their country, he managed to secure a place on the last icebreaker to run for freedom to Leith in Scotland. Schwitters' fellow passengers and wartime refugees included both the Norwegian Royal Family and members of the government – influential company indeed for a German Dadaist refugee with poetic inclinations.

On arrival at Leith however, the free-spirited artist received a cordial, but typical of its time, welcome.

"Hamish! What have we got here?" a Scottish harbour policeman exclaimed to a colleague, whilst collaring the German, "Another guest of King George if I'm not very much mistaken."

And so began Schwitters' journey towards detention behind barbed wire on the Isle of Man as one of 'His Majesty's Most Loyal Enemy Aliens', the official title for internees. Prisoners were suspected of being potential 'sleeper' spies and 'fifth columnists' until a clean refugee pedigree was established.

During World War II there were several internment and prisoner of war camps on the island. Schwitters, together with a wide cross-section of European academics, intellectuals and artists, was detained in one of the 49 boarding houses requisitioned through compulsory eviction orders served on the sitting tenants. This barbed wire enclosed compound became the Hutchinson Square Camp.

With little to occupy their time, the cohort of talented and scholarly inmates established an in-house *academe* to share knowledge freely with other internees. Many enjoyed a better education at the Hutchinson Square 'university' than they would ever have gleaned elsewhere, even during peacetime.

The camp's academic opportunities may have been unparalleled, but the bizarre mood which pervaded the boarding houses was eerily challenging. Internees lived within an aquatic azure gloom during the daylight hours and a pinkish-red bordello glimmer in the hours of darkness. All window panes were painted blue and all clear electric light bulbs were replaced with red globes. This wartime security measure was to prevent potential Nazi infiltrators signalling flickering-light coded messages to any German submarines that may have been lurking expectantly in Douglas Bay.

Wartime austerity made conventional art materials hard to come by, particularly for use by one of His Majesty's Most Loyal Enemy Aliens. The blue window panes were too tempting for artists to ignore and soon pictures were etched onto the painted glass. In no time, the linoleum was stripped away from the floors and used to make linocut masters, leaving behind plain wooden boards.

Amongst the diverse group of internees was the talented concert pianist, Marjan Rawicz, who later became half of the world-famous piano duo, Rawicz and Landauer. Marjan, while endeavouring to coax Steinway-like volume and tonal brilliance from the battered upright boarding house, honky-tonk pianos, was reputed to have left many pianos collapsed or destroyed – martyred to his formidably muscular melodic mode.

The internees attended concerts given by talented musicians, some of whom would later go on to form the world-renowned Amadeus Quartet. Internment may have afforded only a meagre existence, but scholastically it was hard to beat. Within that eminent group, the celebrated Kurt Schwitters was appointed Head of the Cultural Department.

During his career, Schwitters worked in a wide range of art forms and materials, and felt no compunction to have his work sanctified by fashion or the limiting tenets of modernism. He believed abstract art to be a perfectly valid form of expression, but only one amongst many. Landscape and portraiture were equally important, providing formal rigour and discipline to his work. Schwitters was never one to genuflect at the altar of an artistic *ism* or be subverted by the dictates of a faddish clique's manifesto.

With limited materials available he improvised, concentrating on collage works made of found and discarded materials – tickets, newsprint, bottle tops, and all manner of litter. From this refuse he produced a series of extraordinary works which later became highly regarded and much sought-after by collectors and galleries.

Schwitters wasted no time during the sixteen months he spent on the island and produced between 200 and 250 works including landscapes and commissioned portraits.

Portraits were painted at a price of £3 to £5, depending upon compositional requirements. In 2014, a large early 1920's collage work by Schwitters sold at a Christie's auction for $24 million.

What an unexpected honour and delight it was to have the unique and mystifying artworks of Willie Leece displayed alongside those of so distinguished and creative a free spirit as Kurt Schwitters, a one-time leader of Europe's avant-garde artistic factions.

The range and variety of Willie's artworks encapsulated the quirky imagination and creative flair of an unlikely artist, a quiet and reflective Manx farmer. To the casual observer, these incongruous curios may have appeared merely intriguing or amusing distractions. On closer inspection, a rich array of complexity became apparent, a mystifying introspection which exemplified the ingenuity and wry humour with which this agricultural abstractionist imbued his handiworks.

Although Willie fashioned these artworks for his own amusement from sculptural pieces he found along the roadside, there can be little doubt he wanted others to speculate on his creative endeavours. Magnus was fortunate to recognise these unique artistic curios for what they were, and photograph as many as he could find before they were destroyed by the ravages of time or agricultural necessity.

The random events that propelled Willie Leece's innovations from dusty obscurity to the exalted heights of a joint showing at so extraordinary an exhibition also paid dividends to the photographer. Magnus was invited to submit selected artworks for the Sayle Gallery's 2013 Christmas Exhibition.

His contributions comprised three coastal landscapes in oils and, in keeping with the Schwitters/Leece tradition, two collages made of found materials – *Nasty Mouth, The Tattooed Redskin*, and *Tufty Geek, A Person of Wiry Puzzlement*. Much to his surprise, the collages created a good deal of furrowed-browed hilarity, particularly amongst the young. This heartening reaction spurred Magnus on to create two additional collages – *Commander Benedict Forksbeard, The Startled Speed Reader* and *Señor Longnose Peggchin, The Sentimental Viking Poet*.

Both *Forksbeard* and *Peggchin* have an origin that is utterly random and accidental, a slow and haphazard evolution dependent upon when their bits were found and how the fragments were arranged.

There was however nothing accidental about their given names. These were instant and obvious thanks to lucky beachcomber finds. A length of hairy rope, a long strip of sea-bleached blue plastic and a bald half tennis ball gave rise to both their conception and titles. Of course, embedded meaning and ascribed personality, the supplement to their names, had to wait until the works were fully formed and identifiable.

Both creations were christened on the sands of Port Soif, a seaside inlet on Guernsey, one of the Channel Islands, where these fragments were found. At the time, Magnus was holidaying there with his elder daughter Willow Victoria and her family who for six years abandoned Australia to take up residency on the island.

Magnus believed the newer collages to be more eye-catching and intriguing than the earlier *Nasty Mouth* and *Tufty Geek*, so he took the plunge of entering the more recent works in the 2014 Summer Exhibition in London's Royal Academy of Arts. This action wasn't the result of a sudden blooming of self-confidence or hubris, but simply by adopting the go-getting philosophy he'd taken to heart in Australia, 'Av-a-go-yer-mug'.

So *Commander Benedict Forksbeard* and *Señor Longnose Peggchin* were entered for the 2014 Summer Exhibition. Of the 14000 or so entries, only about 1200 are hung for public viewing; that's less than a one in ten chance of making the final cut, long odds for a self-taught 70-year-old amateur artist in competition with hungry professionals, many of whom were distinguished members of the international art fraternity. It was pure Schwitters rub-off and a wish to challenge fortune that buoyed him to vie for hanging space alongside such an august clique of insiders.

The Royal Academy of Arts is one of the few organisations in the world that is run by artists, so the selection panel comprises artists sitting in judgement on artists. Entries are initially pared down to around 2000 works by scrutinising digital images. The final selection to be hung is made by reviewing the actual artworks.

Recent research at Harvard University concluded that truly creative individuals, by virtue of their very nature, tend to ignore rules more readily than staid, unimaginative types. The study implied that those with an inspired artistic bent, who abandon tradition in striving for originality, may cultivate rebellious traits and so disregard social norms and challenge convention, as did Pablo Picasso and the anti-retinal joker, Marcel Duchamp. Arty types might err on the side of anarchy and may have few qualms in flouting the law to follow in the footsteps of Tom Keating, perhaps the most prolific art forger of the twentieth century. If this is the case, could it be that the Summer Exhibition at the Royal

Academy is little more than a colourful meeting place where the creatively dishonest display their copies and fakes whilst thumbing their collective noses at the rest of the populace? Probably not, for there were at least two works, *Commander Benedict Forksbeard* and *Señor Longnose Peggchin*, that were in every way original and in which each item of their assemblage was rummaged for or found, not pilfered. They were inspirational works by an original thinker, as no doubt were most of the other exhibits, and not the work of robbers, cheats, liars or fraudsters.

It was never clear whether it was the down-in-the-mouth gloominess of *Señor Longnose Peggchin* or the flabbergasted bewilderment of *Commander Benedict Forksbeard* that stirred the Royal Academy selection panel's callousness, for both collages were to be hung – not at the Royal Academy next to Grayson Perry's embroidered tapestries or Una Stubbs' water colours of Benedict Cumberbatch (Sherlock Holmes) and Martin Freeman (Dr Watson) – but hung by the neck. Both works were given the finger at the first digital hurdle.

The £25 entry fee however, was firmly grasped. The Royal Academy receives about £350,000 in fees from entries. With so many hopefuls, only a brief time may be allocated to accept or reject each entry. Assume ten seconds to review each digital image, giving a pay rate of £9,000 an hour – good business if you can get it. It's worth noting however that the entry fees don't support the judges' high life, but provide scholarship funding for budding artists.

All was not lost. As with the Archibald portrait competition in Australia which, like the Royal Academy Summer Exhibition, is open to all-comers, entries which just missed out on being hung may be made available for public viewing. *Benedict* and *Longnose* were given an airing in the Parish of Kirk Onchan Library on the Isle of Man.

The local Librarian staged an exhibition for ten of Magnus's paintings and collages, and as hoped, the local kids were fascinated by the collages as they could identify toothpaste cap eyes, fast-food fork teeth or clothes peg beards. Like Willie Leece, Magnus also enjoyed having his artworks on public display. Even the Island's Westminster representative, the Lieutenant Governor (and his wife) dropped in for a viewing.

Understandably, Magnus's future was not radically changed by the artworks exhibited at the local library. The most unexpected and enduring impact upon his future life resulted from the arbitrary act of inviting his sister, Susan Maureen, to view the Schwitters exhibition at the Sayle Gallery. Who would have thought that so innocent an act would result in the unearthing of a missing masterpiece created by the twentieth century's hardest working and greatest artistic genius?

But more of this later …

Chapter 7 – The Pilgrim

****

At present we know only that the imagination,
like certain wild animals,
will not breed in captivity.

George Orwell (1903 – 1950)

The Preservation of Literature

****

Old age need not preclude adventure. In retirement, one of Magnus's greatest pleasures was long distance walking along paths and trails that he knew little or nothing about. Some trekkers conduct detailed research to become familiar with where they're going and what they might see along the way. No doubt planning is essential for off the beaten tracks or potentially dangerous trails. For the countryside Magnus liked to explore, he needed only the most basic knowledge of where the trail led, and that there had been no near-by outbreaks of cannibalism or the like, to cause concern. Freedom of the open road is magical, the unexpected both challenging and enlivening. It must be confessed though, that most of the tedious research for the trails he'd tramped had been done by others. Magnus's meagre contribution, like that of the film character Chauncey Gardiner, was just 'Being There' with enough money to pay his way, resilient good humour and a stout pair of boots to keep tramping.

He'd been so inspired by the miraculous transformation of his disposition after tramping Alfred Wainwright's celebrated trail across the north of England during the autumn of 2005 that he wrote a book about the experience.

During the spring of 2014, he and an Australian mate, Clive, tramped a trail from France into Spain. The trail headed westward from St-Jean-Pied-du-Port across the undulating foothills of the French Pyrenees, and onwards through the Basque Mountains to Bilbao, an ancient Spanish seaport with access to the Bay of Biscay.

The mountainous terrain was made for hard trekking, but the rewards were mighty – fresh air, physical exertion, open countryside and arriving each evening at an unfamiliar oasis where the food and wine were generally good and plentiful.

Each morning brought with it the delight of walking away from the day before, leaving cares behind, carrying only what was required. During the 12-day, 250km hike, Magnus and Clive experienced many light-hearted adventures, and were endlessly enchanted by the majestic vistas. The escapade still stirs a warm glow of overall satisfaction in his being and, amongst the plethora of extraordinary events that occurred, three particularly memorable incidents arise.

On the first full day's walk in Spain – their fifth on the road – a mystical ember sparked and rekindled Magnus's long forgotten curiosity about mental telepathy, extra sensory perception and the allure of shapely legs that keep going up and up.

The day's route followed the coast from the French/Spanish border town of Irun to the busy seaport of San Sebastian. The trail, part of The Northern Caminos, is one of the famous pilgrimage paths to the cathedral of Santiago de Compostela, a route favoured in the late Middle Ages by pilgrims from the British Isles.

About noon they arrived at the seaport and former naval harbour of Pasajes de San Juan. They entered from the east along a narrow, cobbled harbour side way lined with ancient warehouses, many converted to stylish, waterside restaurants. Both he and Clive were ready for lunch but not eager for a full meal so, as wayfarers and pilgrims had done for a millennium or more, they boarded the ferry to cross the harbour.

The ship repair slipways and fishing paraphernalia that cluttered the work-a-day western harbourside left little space for restaurants. There was however, a fisherman's café; a simple grotto seemingly hewn out of the cliff face. It was starkly plain in the bright sunshine outside, whilst inside it was small and lightless grey, like a 1930's film set for weary seadogs on shore leave. The back and side walls were roughly worked, and left at that. Tatty crab pots and other fishing tackle dangled from above and hung out from the rock walls. Swarthy, casually-dressed seafarers and their womenfolk lounged on old metal chairs, cradling wine glasses and eating medallions of fish whilst talking quietly – a wonderful, authentic local find where Magnus felt immediately at home.

They secured the last available table, by the rock wall next to a chest freezer, alongside the tiny kitchen in which an attractive woman in her early fifties skilfully sliced a skinned dogfish into small steaks ready for batter and frying.

"Fish OK?" said Magnus to Clive, nodding to what other diners were eating.

"Ideal," Clive replied.

"Pardon Madame. Possibilitemont deux portion de poisson ici, si vous plait?" Magnus concocted in garbled French, pointing at the slices of dogfish.

"No Señor, poisson fini," she replied.

"Think again Clive," he said. "The fish is off."

At that moment, another woman appeared through the kitchen, just in front of Magnus.

"Today's catch is finished. But there is tuna available," she said to Clive in perfect, if accented, English.

Standing close, she looked around at Magnus and their eyes locked in startled surprise. A thrilling jolt of recognition surged between them which was so intense he felt sure they'd both stopped breathing, as deep within their eyes two souls became one. She was in her late thirties, possibly forty, and disconcertingly beautiful with a mane of lustrous black hair. Full of shocked acknowledgement, they slowly smiled into each other's faces as though they'd known each other for years and very much liked what they knew; and yet they'd never met. How odd life is. Two strangers meet in a quayside grotto, sense fancy at first flush, simply because the dogfish was off and with only tuna on the menu.

The transcendental fluency of their mutual attraction reinforced Magnus's suspicion about the existence of, and occasional engagement with, a not widely acknowledged, mysterious sixth sense – a form of insight that is intuitive, instinctive and instant, to which they'd both responded, and which may not be readily suppressed. Magnus believed that their shared awareness challenged the scientific mindset which espouses certainty that life and consciousness are mere chemical reactions devoid of any clairvoyant substance.

She was busy serving customers as the two trekkers left the café. Magnus hung back to wave goodbye; she turned and saw him, and her smile, a radiant source of happiness in a mutually recognised and understood secret, remained with him.

Magnus and Clive's trekking adventure ended in Bilbao, although for serious pilgrims the trail stretched 650 km further to the cathedral of Santiago de Compostela. Whilst it would have been a true taste of outdoor freedom to carry on, Clive had to return Down Under for work, and in truth, although Magnus enjoyed what they'd done, he had no great desire to go further.

He was however, tempted to return to the fish café and see if the spark that had flashed there could be fanned into a true flame of romantic excitement. On reflection, he didn't go. His reticence didn't stem from the age difference alone. At the time he wasn't wired for romance, but for life support. Some months earlier Magnus had been treated in hospital for an enlarged prostate, and remained amorously encumbered with an implanted catheter; a tube which enabled him to pass water.

In 1997, King Juan Carlos of Spain inaugurated Bilbao's cubist inspired Guggenheim Museum, a cultural shrine at which art lovers and the 'aesthetically engaged' go to pay homage. Magnus and Clive made the most of their opportunity to visit the titanium-clad treasure house and were inspired by what they saw

It was obvious why the monumental walk-through sculptures by the American, Richard Serra, with their unadulterated rolled steel patina, are permanently installed in the pride-of-place ground floor gallery. If they'd been located on an elevated level, their combined floor-load may have brought the whole edifice tumbling down.

The quirky creative flare of the Brazilian artist, Ernesto Neto, was engagingly expressed through his gallery-wide crochet spider-web spice-scented assemblages and the 30 metre dangling organic enclosures of sensual see-through droplets.

Yoko Ono's *Half-A-Wind Show: A Retrospective*, organised to coincide with her 80th birthday, required the entire top floor of the gallery to encapsulate the essence of her life's work. Ono's (and John Lennon's) mantra, *The Power of Imagination*, and was hypnotically exemplified in *The Clock*, a 24 hour long video piece by Christian Marclay. The video is made up of snippets from thousands of black and white films, ingeniously spliced and edited so that the unrelated segments of the 'story' are set at the actual time of day the viewer is watching. Magnus tried to buy a copy, but it's not available on general release, being restricted for art gallery use only.

The two walkers left Spain via tourist-choked Barcelona, Clive departing after one day for Australia, and Magnus several days later for the Isle of Man.

Whilst alone, Magnus avoided crowded tourist haunts, although he couldn't resist paying homage at the altar of a creative wunderkind by visiting the Picasso Museum, where he let himself down badly. After half an hour of suffering the grating voices of the shrill American beauties, with their straight blond hair, expensive perfume, stratospheric ambition and perfect teeth, who were right behind his neck in the queue for entry tickets, he was forced into an act of mental self-preservation. He turned to the 'film star' at his elbow and, emulating their volume, asked smiling, "Excuse me, is it your breath that whiffs of garlic, or is it mine?" And with that, silence and sanity was restored, although he was filled with remorse.

He also visited the Maritime Museum, which included a tour of *Santa Eulalia*, a three-masted schooner made fast to the quayside. The sailing ship had a long and honourable history trading between

Mediterranean ports. As an ageing vessel she became engaged in the less salubrious pursuit of smuggling wheat from Spain to the Balearic Islands. Even though the vessel is 47 metres long, lengthier than both Darwin's HMS *Beagle* and Captain Bligh's HMS *Bounty*, everything, including the cargo hold, seemed small and cluttered with shipboard paraphernalia. The whiffs of shipboard life – hemp rope, tar, recently worked wood, linseed oil, salt, diesel fuel and paint – all seemed eerily familiar to Magnus. The steep companionway in the vessel's prow which gave access to the cramped fo'c'sle cabin, a wedge-shaped slot and home to four members of the ship's crew, particularly excited his memory.

Faster than the speed of light, the smells, taste, feel, sound and sight of that claustrophobic dungeon whisked Magnus back over forty years, to his mid-twenties, when he nearly signed on as crew/engineer aboard just such a sailing ship with equally airless crew quarters. At that time, his reason for not taking passage aboard the *Golden Cachalote*, was not that he wasn't attracted to the adventure of following Charles Darwin's voyage to the Galapagos Islands, but that he needed to earn a living. Also, the prospect of swimming amongst shoals of hammerhead sharks, which seemed such a major selling point to other crew members, inspired him not one jot.

"What's the pay?" Magnus asked the skipper and part owner of the schooner.

"Sixteen pounds a month," he replied, "and you have to repatriate yourself to the UK if you choose to pay-off."

As a graduate trainee with Hawker Siddeley, he had little money and couldn't call on family backing to augment his meagre income. The rug had been pulled out from under the McAulay family fortunes in 1939, at the outbreak of the Second World War, and was dashed to pieces during the spring of 1948. The Galapagos escapade was waived in favour of the lucky few able to afford it.

In 1939, the newly married Arthur Wilfred (Wilf), Magnus's father, was running his own motor bike and cycling business on the Isle of Man, and had been doing so since his 22nd birthday. His Athol Street premises were only a few doors removed from where his future wife's relatives ran their Robinson Bros printing business, the onetime publishers of *Robinson's Sporting Tissue*, and sometime printer of the Manx Government's *Tynwald Hansard*. Wilfred's promising commercial career was no sooner firing smoothly on all cylinders than it stalled due to Adolf Hitler's hostile takeover bid for parts of Eastern Europe. How odd it is, that the maniacal ambitions of a failed Austrian artist could so profoundly scupper the endeavours of a young entrepreneurial Manxman a thousand miles away – hardly the butterfly's wing effect, but equally whimsical. Wilf's business was forced to close when war was declared; the motorcycles were requisitioned for the war effort; and, due to his trade, Wilf was enrolled into non-combat, reserved occupation building the 27 litre Merlin Spitfire engines at a Rolls Royce factory in England. During the Battle of Britain, Wilf was one amongst the thousands of ground crew working round-the-clock to keep Spitfire and Hurricane fighter planes in the air to fend off the Nazi Luftwaffe on their bombing runs to destroy RAF airfields and industry estates, and to shake the stiff-necked resolve of the British people.

At the end of that war, when discharged from reserved occupation, he returned to civilian life on the Isle of Man with his wife, Margaret Lillian, and their family of three small children, the youngest of whom was Magnus. Thanks to the mighty German Blitzkrieg, housing in Britain was difficult to come by. The Isle of Man was no exception and the McAulay clan was fortunate to find a farm-labourer's wooded hut in which to live.

During the early 1920's, the demountable hut had been relocated to the corner of a field on Bibaloe Beg Farm, flanking the McAulay's tribal territory of Lonan Parish. During The Great War (1914-1918) the cabin had been home to some of the 20,000 German, Austrian and Turkish Prisoners of War and civilian internees confined in the Knockaloe Moar Internment Camp for the duration of that conflict.

No sooner had the family moved into the leaky-roofed, former prison camp hut, than their father was conscripted into the RAF for two years compulsory National Service. He spent most of this time on the chilly Hebrides, an archipelago of bleak islands which, in Viking times, had been part of The Kingdom of Mann and Isles, a realm which stretched from the northwest coast of Scotland into the Irish Sea to include the Isle of Man. On these remote Scottish islands, Wilf decommissioned military airfields, their purpose having ended with Hitler's suicide and Germany's surrender.

In late 1947, Arthur Wilfred returned home to recommence a normal family and business life in his homeland. His first action was to move the family from the Bibaloe Beg prison camp hut, laughably registered as Bibaloe Bungalow, to Robin's Croft, a tiny stone farm-labourer's cottage nestling on the edge of Fairy Glen, near the Pot-n-Pan waterfall on the Groudle River, in the postal district of Kerrowdhoo. The cottage came with enough land for a large chicken run to provide additional income, Wilf's primary occupation being that of motorcycle mechanic.

At Robin's Croft, for the first time in his life, Magnus had a playmate of his own age. Andrew lived in Glen Rosa, the only house close by. Andrew was lucky because his home nestled beneath the foliage of the Fairy Glen trees and from his bedroom he could listen to the tumbling waters of the nearby waterfall.

When they were five years old, Magnus and Andrew were often driven to school in Andrew's father's car. Cars were few and far between in those days of post-war deprivation; however, it was necessary transport for Andrew's father to conduct his business as a dealer in rabbit skins and feathers.

In Poland, before World War II, Andrew's father had been a talented taxidermist kept busy preparing, stuffing and mounting the dead pets and hunting trophies of the Polish aristocracy and eager-to-impress social climbers. He arrived in Britain in the late 1930's where he volunteered to joined the RAF to fight the common enemy, the German Nazis.

In the late 1950's, Andrew's family moved from Glen Rosa to open a guesthouse at Hague Farm (the manor house in which Captain Bligh's fiancé lived prior to their wedding in 1781). One of their summer guests was a wealthy Scottish Laird who persuaded Andrew's mother to become his housekeeper-come-cook, and her taxidermist husband to reinvent himself as his gamekeeper, a job in which he could use his considerable expertise with dead creatures and their skins. So the family moved to Scotland and Magnus lost contact with Andrew.

In no time things were looking up at Robin's Croft, especially for the three small children. The place was overrun with hens and bantams, and expensive eggs were back on the menu. The children's greatest pleasure was caring for the newly hatched chicks. Fertilized eggs were incubated in a heated wooden barrel alongside which the newly-hatched chicks were kept warm.

The children's mother, Margaret Lillian, contributed to the success of the enterprise by collecting eggs from the chicken run and hedgerows, where some independently minded chickens preferred to nest and lay, and delivering the eggs on her push-bike to a village grocer for sale.

Conditions at their new home were primitive at best. Downstairs lighting was by pressurised paraffin mantle-lamps, with candle light upstairs. Cooking and heating water was on primus stoves and the coal fire. There was no bathroom, but there was cold running water to the washing-up sink. An enamel bowl on the kitchen table was used for personal washing and at weekends the grubby children took turns to luxuriate in a galvanised tin bath in front of the coal fire. The lavatory for daytime use was an outdoor thunder-box in a lean-to which housed an enamel bucket under a wooden bench-seat with a large hole cut through. The small children were unduly anxious about falling through the bench-seat hole into the guano below. Chamber pots were used during the night.

Even though the cottage was little more than a rustic hovel, Margaret Lilian and Arthur Wilfred were eager to brighten up the whitewashed stone walls of their new home. Post-war austerity left little cash for necessities, let alone the luxury of interior decoration. Huddled around the kitchen fire on a bitterly cold December night, when cheerily charged with pre-Christmas Rich Ruby port wine, the young couple hit upon a decoration idea that was within their means.

They cleared the kitchen and covered the knobby, concrete floor with old newspapers (kept for lighting the fire), then set about their task in a merry atmosphere of Rich Ruby charged abandonment. Taking turns, they hurling an old tennis ball, pre-soaked in pea green distemper, at the whitewashed walls. On impact, the luminous paint spattered everywhere creating unique patterns the like of which may have made the American Abstract Expressionist drip-painter, Jackson Pollock, raise an eyebrow in admiration.

Unbeknownst to Wilfred and Margaret, they had created a new style of kinetic performance art which for ever imprinted itself on the receptive mind of their three-year-old son, Magnus, and which later would be acknowledged in select circles as Manx nouveau réalisme. During the early 1960's, the avant-garde French artist, Yves Klein, thought he was well ahead of the game with a publicity-seeking happening in which he invited three naked girls to act as 'living paintbrushes' to smear pigment, daubed on their breasts, bellies, thighs and bottoms, on to large vertical surfaces. Little did Klein know, but over a decade earlier, at Robin's Croft, in the postal district of Kerrowdhoo, a young Manx couple had already set a high bar for performance art which, in some minds, the Frenchman's postmodernist minge-art failed to better.

Even though most things were in short supply and wartime food rationing would remain for many more years, the McAulay family's livelihood had taken a turn for the better. They'd all survived the war, had a roof over their heads that didn't leak, didn't go hungry, and were warm indoors during winter. They benefited from two incomes – meagre though they were – and the children, like the chickens, were free-range, happy with acres of countryside and Fairy Glen to play in.

The blue touch-paper of their parents' commercial ambitions had been reignited, albeit with a slow-burn. It wasn't long however, before those glowing embers of aspiration were stifled, then doused in an instant.

On the evening of Friday 5th March 1948, Magnus was at home in Robin's Croft with his father. At three and a half years old, he was too young to go to the cinema with his mother, brother and sister. The mile-long rural walk from Robin's Croft to Onchan's Avenue Cinema, was nothing new. His five-year-old brother and seven-year-old sister walked it every school day when they didn't ride on their father's motor bike. James Arthur Radcliff sat up front between his father's outstretched arms to the handle bars, with his legs dangling on each side of the petrol tank, and Susan Maureen sat behind as a pillion passenger, clinging to her father's waist.

Mostly they walked to school along quiet country roads. Sometimes it was foggy and they strode through the swirling mist with ghostly trees and bushes on either side. On such days, Susan Maureen counted her footsteps between the blasts of the foghorn on Douglas Head, three miles away. Each time the sum was fifty-nine steps – never sixty. Susan, a pupil in Miss Pedder's class, was awarded a wall-chart gold star for times-tables and sums.

Wrapped up against the winter chill, the three cinema goers trooped through the evening gloaming, expecting to return two hours later, chatting merrily about the film in the frosty pitch-black night, with only the unnerving undergrowth crunch of the foraging nocturnal wildlife for company.

Much to their delight, they met Aunty Winnie, their mother's sister Winifred Agnes, alighting from a bus in Onchan Village.

"Winnie!" exclaimed their mother. "What a surprise."

"Oh Margaret," cried Winnie, clearly upset and carrying a suitcase. "I've had enough of Jack Prince. I've left him, and am on my way to you."

There were no pictures and ice creams that night, just the uphill drag back to Robin's Croft lugging the suitcase and a crock of Winnie's sad memories along with them. During her marriage to the former policeman, P.C. Jack Prince, Winnie endured the loss of five babies, either miscarriages or stillborn, reputedly as a result of complications brought on by her husband denying her proper medical attention during her first pregnancy.

Saturday morning broke bright and frosty-brittle, but Robin's Croft was warm and alive to the excited shrieking of three children bouncing on a bed and wrestling their favourite aunt, Winnie.

"If you don't stop jumping on the bed, you'll break the springs," their father called out laughingly, sitting astride a dilapidated, pre-war motor bike, waiting in the chilly winter air to be push-started. He paddled forward with his feet whilst his wife, Margaret Lillian, trotted behind pushing. He let in the clutch, the engine fired, and he chugged off to work and into the Never-Never, leaving his young wife rubbing her hands together for warmth.

Wilf's cousin, Morewood, lived in Sunnyside, a cottage a few hundred yards up the road from Robin's Croft. On that morning, Morewood's wife, Ruth, a former milliner, was in bed recovering from child birth two weeks earlier and was being visited by her sister, Jean.

"Seeing you, Jean, always cheers me up," said Ruth.

Jean stood by her sister's bedroom window looking out at the frigid, skeletal-treed morning wondering what to say. Finding comforting words for the loss of a new born baby is no easy task, particularly for a tragedy that was entirely avoidable. Ruth had opted to use a private clinic for her second confinement to avoid the fate which had befallen Barbara, their first born. Barbara was spastic, having suffered oxygen starvation at birth. Ruth's second child, Pauline, was perfect, a beautiful healthy baby, but she lived for only ten days. Through neglect or oversight, alone in a cot, the baby choked to death on her mother's regurgitated milk.

The silent wintery stillness of Sunnyside Cottage on Little Mill Road was broken by the easy throb of a single cylinder motor bike accelerating along the empty country road.

"There goes Wilf off to work," said Jean, glad of the distraction, until a moment later, "Oh! He's fallen off the bike."

"Is he alright?" asked Ruth anxiously. "Has he got up?"

"No!" Jean cried. "He's still lying on the road."

Jean and Morewood, who was downstairs, rushed along the road to help their cousin, but it was no use. As was usual at the time, Wilf hadn't been wearing his horsehair crash helmet and had fractured his skull.

It's true the weakest link in a chain usually parts first. Whether or not that was the case with their father's motorbike chain will remain a mystery. What is known however is that the chain parted, but instead of streaming onto the road, as is generally the case with a broken chain, it snatched and wrapped around the back wheel drive sprocket, flipping the motorcycle and rider into the air.

Arthur Wilfred died at four that afternoon leaving a widow, three children and their favourite aunt to get by in Robin's Croft, a dark and damp eighteenth century farm worker's cottage with no sanitation, gas or electricity, and most pressingly, no income apart from that gleaned selling hens' eggs.

During two busy weeks that March, Morewood was crushed by the emotional burden of attending coronial inquests and funerals, one of each for his new born baby daughter, Pauline, and again for his cousin, Arthur Wilfred.

Philosophers and mathematicians may argue that pure rationality is irrefutable and cannot be challenged. Some anthropologists may however, disagree. For instance, in the desert kingdom of Saudi Arabia, if a taxi is involved in an accident, the passenger is usually blamed – not the driver. The upturned reasoning behind this seemingly anarchical verdict is that, had the passenger not hired the taxi, the vehicle would have been elsewhere, and therefore the accident couldn't have occurred.

By relating this rickety rationale to 'what if' history, it is not unreasonable to imagine that had the young Adolf Hitler been encouraged to pursue his early dream of becoming an artist with more determination, and become as successful as Kurt Schwitters, his whole life may have been different. Had this transpired it's not beyond the realms of possibility that Hitler's formidable energy may have been channelled into artistic pursuits rather than scheming to establish and then lead the Third Reich – thus perhaps avoiding World War II?

This speculation raises the question, had Hitler pursued an alternative career, would

Magnus's father have been killed riding to work on a chilly March morning in 1948? The answer must surely be no, for he'd have been elsewhere, involved with other issues. From the time of being drafted into the war effort in 1939, his life would have been utterly different. And, in all probability, Susan Maureen, James Arthur Radcliffe and Magnus Henry would never have been conceived.

Hitler's abandoned artistic ambitions cannot be held responsible for the children's existence, nor used as an excuse for anything that befell them in life. In Magnus's case, the path chosen in the spring of 2014 was trekking through the Basque countryside of France and Spain, and it was in the famous red chilli pepper province of that landscape where he was destined to experience the second of the memorable incidents of the walk.

Chapter 8 – The Aficionado

****

I am always doing that which I cannot do,
in order that I may learn how to do it.

Pablo Picasso (1881 – 1973)

****

The epidemic was localised. French law and officious bureaucrats made sure of that. The infection was lawfully isolated according to the dictates of *appellation d'origine controlee (AOC)* – controlled designation of origin. Many of the buildings in the tight-knit rural Basque township of Espelette appeared to be suffering from a nasty red rash on their outer walls. But as is so often the case, all was not as it seemed. The buildings weren't covered in a lumpy blight, but long strings of the capsicum genus, members of the nightshade family.

The colourful fruits were there to dry in the sun whilst advertising the local highly protected industry, the famous Espelette red chilli peppers. Basque cuisine would be indistinguishable from other regional foodstuff if not for the inclusion of this prized local ingredient.

Clive and Magnus arrived in Espelette on the second day of their walk through France. They'd covered 40km of the 250km trek and were happily getting into the swing of things. There's always a lot to learn at the beginning of a long distance trek; one lesson they'd forgotten however, was always to treat certain native knowledge with a large pinch of salt.

They'd been lost only once, and that was thanks to specific directions from a local motorist who'd screeched his car to a halt to give them assistance they didn't need; the map they were consulting showed perfectly well which way to go. Foolishly, they took the Frenchman's advice and suffered an hour of confused anxiety, wondering where on earth they were.

Being lost undermined their confidence in their navigational abilities and tended to erode the beneficial effects of a life on the open road. The disgruntled trekkers were eventually rescued when they flagged down the only vehicle they met on the empty back road. Their saviours were greatly amused at the antics of the agitated foreigners who tried to explain their predicament by repeatedly exclaiming 'Espelette! Espelette! through the driver's window. After a great deal of merriment, the Basque mother and son understood their plight and loaded the hikers into the back of the battered van amongst a stack of paint drums and stained rags. The van clattered and snaked around narrow country lanes until they were dropped off at a crossroads where a wooden signpost finger had the welcome name, Espelette, carved into it. Laughing wildly, their rescuer slammed the battered Citron into gear and trundled off, waving goodbye and shouting '*bonne chance*' to the disoriented Anglo-Saxon/Australians.

Their Espelette hotel was a traditional rustic Basque building with its interior recently refurbished in a starkly restrained fashion. The middle-aged landlady was stylish and shapely, but it was her mannerisms that distinguished her from all other hoteliers they met along the way. She was all affectation and flowing hand gestures, nothing hard-edged. Her clothes were figure hugging, but oddly tweedy. Even with her elaborate Sybil Fawlty style bouffant hair, she definitely wore the trousers in that hotel; and yet, in a teasingly corseted way, she was vibratingly sexy.

She preceded them up the staircase to their room which, much to their surprise, was not a twin share, but contained a double bed.

"This can't be right," Clive spluttered uncertainly.

"It's not," Magnus stated producing the booking slip. "Here's confirmation of our booking, and it's for a twin share, not a double."

"Oh!" exclaimed the landlady in a flurry of extravagant hand fluttering, head wobbling, eyelid widening and lip pursing gestures. "We av all sorts ear," she apologised, with her head on one side, play-acting contrition, whilst her eyes twinkled with impish glee. "Ow was I to know?"

She put matters right, allocating better rooms than they'd booked – two single rooms for the price of a twin share. Thank goodness there'd be no bed-sharing that night and, happily, red-faced embarrassment was avoided all round.

That evening her desire to spruik the hotel's cuisine and confirm her close personal control of everything in the dining room was plain to see. Very much the *maître d'hôtel*, she arrived three steps behind their main course, then proceeded to enlighten the diners in the bare essentials of French cuisine, whilst the neglected food cooled.

"Ear we av the French bean, ear le French green pea, ici the carrot and voilà, le dookling foot," she explained, gesturing lovingly to each item of food with the exaggerated flourish of a scantily-clad conjuror's assistant distracting the onlookers from the deception taking place before their very eyes.

The fare reflected the dining room's décor – minimalist and meagre. When she waved across the pea she got it just right; there was only a single limp snow pea on each plate, although to be fair, there was a sprinkling of beans.

It wasn't only Magnus and Clive who were somewhat disappointed by the size of the meal. A large, three generations, family party sitting at the next table made their dissatisfaction absolutely clear. The elderly patriarch in the group went to great animated lengths to express his displeasure at the measly size of their meals. Only a single word, *microscopique*, was necessary to gauge his meaning.

It would seem that it's not just dyed-in-the-wool roast beef and Yorkshire pudding Britons who find *nouvelle cuisine* wanting; some Frenchmen are inclined to agree.

Espelette remained firmly engrained in Magnus's memory, not for the red chilli pepper bejewelled houses, nor for the captivating mannerisms of their landlady, or even because of the tedium of wasting an hour setting off to walk eastwards instead of westwards when leaving the town. What captured his attention and remains very active in his psyche resulted from a casual diversion when looking for a post box on the morning of their departure.

It must have been market day, for the shopping mall was busy and lined with inviting street stalls selling local produce – mainly red chilli peppers in every guise imaginable, supplemented by the lesser known local delicacy of sheep's cheese. The shops had opened early to attract the passing trade which, even before breakfast, was bustling.

"La poste, s'il vous plait Monsieur," Magnus asked the shopkeeper across from the hotel.

"Ici," he replied cheerfully, pointing to the yellow post box.

On that cool, bright morning, the convivial atmosphere amongst the early shoppers and traders was wonderfully infectious. Magnus posted the letters before ambling back to the shop which offered irresistible browsing, being brim-full of bric-a-brac and antiques. He had no intention of buying anything as his backpack was already heavy enough, and over 200 kilometres of rugged tramping still lay ahead.

At the back of the shop, on a chair seat, alongside stacks of dusty furniture and a red-rusty, two-metre-tall cast iron Jesus, a grubby heavily glazed ceramic plate caught Magnus's eye. Once in his hands he knew instantly what he was holding. He was exhilarated by the thrill of discovery. Everything about the find screamed of a legendary artist's wizardry.

The plate depicted a medieval knight, armed with a halberd, clad in a plumed golden helmet with matching tunic, standing before a backward facing bottle-green horse sporting a wildly streaming tail. The steed's halter, bridle and cloak were festooned with exotic bejewelled motifs. Both knight and mount were exquisitely executed and decorated with a flourish of white, gold, chocolate and lime green studs and amulets, contrasted against a luminous blue ground. A self-assured display of bold brushwork perfectly captured the knight's demeanour to radiate a gritty individuality. The fluent execution of the brilliantly conceived work, and its dazzling chromatic imagery, reflected the gifts of a playful artistic genius.

Magnus's heart pounded, his hands trembled; he could hardly contain himself. What a find! What a souvenir! What luck!

"What is your best price for the plate?" he asked the dealer, trying desperately to conceal the depth of his interest.

The antique trader reviewed a ledger before stating, "In Biarritz, I pay 100 euro, you av for 130."

Magnus kept his cool and a price was agreed at a good discount from the original 180-euro price tag. And that's the unlikely and unimaginable sequence of events that led him to become the owner of a superb, 33cm diameter, earthenware plate which he believed exhibited the familiar characteristics of his favourite artist and a twentieth century cultural giant, one Pablo Picasso.

Some may think the price ridiculously low for an original Picasso ceramic, and they'd be right. In 2012, official editions of his ceramic pieces from The Madoura Collection, works of impeccable provenance, sold at a Christie's auction for tens of thousands of euros each, most at over double the estimate. All were factory produced copies, edition pieces made in series ranging from 5 to 500 each. None were works from the hands of Pablo Picasso himself.

If, as Magnus believed, the plate was an original Picasso – neither unique, nor an edition or fake piece – and if both its provenance and authorship could be established with certainty, then the plate would be worth a substantial sum. If not, his 'Picasso' would remain a treasured memento, one which, in years to come, would certainly not find a place on a garage sale table, as is the fate of many souvenirs.

No matter how these exciting thoughts exercised his overwrought brain, his immediate concern was of a more pressing and mundane nature – how to carry the large and fragile treasure along the rough tracks of the Pyrenees foothills without breakage?

"What do you think of this Clive?" he gloated, holding the plate protectively.

"Where did you get it and what's it for?" Clive asked uncertainly. "Won't it be awkward to carry?"

Magnus relived the story over breakfast. It was an agitated and rambling account as his entire emotional and nervous system was alive with the thrilling pleasure of discovering so unique a treasure.

Fortunately, the plate just fitted through the neck of his backpack allowing spare clothes and wet weather gear to be employed as support and protection against chance accidents if he stumbled or fell along the way. A nearly complete copy of a discarded Sunday Times provided additional packaging. With the plate padded inside the newspaper and protected amongst the clothes in the strapped tight backpack, Magnus felt confident it was well cushioned against accidents. He was well aware that the plate was not a typical Picasso ceramic as the detailed finish, rich colouration, and assured modelling reflected the artist's late painting style rather than that of his customary spare ceramic motif.

Picasso mystified those who revere conformity by, repeatedly and unexpectedly, throughout his long and prolific artistic life, producing something atypical – a total revolution in art such as cubism, later collage, or creating a new and liberating painting style. Magnus believed the plate to be one of the occasional *jeux d'esprit* works Picasso fashioned over more than twenty years, producing a continuous stream of unconventional ceramic works.

He was aware of the rare privilege it was to be walking with a Picasso stashed in his backpack; but, with his wonderful find safely shielded between his shoulder blades, he didn't feel as though he was actually walking, but floating several feet off the ground. Even years later, he still hadn't got over the thrill of discovery and the delight in owning a piece of the great man's work.

The treasure on his back wasn't some sort of acolyte's precious relic, like Picasso's fingernail parings or hair clippings, which the artist always kept secure in case they were purloined for shamanic mischief, something he was keen to avoid. What Magnus was keeping close was a prize he believed had The Magician's fingerprints all over it. However, the hard part lay ahead, and that was to prove its creator was indeed the person that his senses, heart, intuition, response and scholarship supposed it to be.

For the remainder of the trek, he was alert to the vulnerability of the fragile object on his back, although the extra care taken on slippery and treacherous terrain didn't slow them down or create any difficulties. During their daily stopovers however, Magnus became somewhat paranoid about the plate being stolen while he and Clive were out-on-the-town hitting the tapas bars. All concern was ill-founded; even airport security procedures and the flights back to the Isle of Man were incident free and he returned there with the plate in one piece and chip free.

Chapter 9 – The Researcher

****

What strip mining is to nature
the art market has become to culture.

Robert Hughes (1938 – 2012)

Art critic, writer and television producer

****

Establishing the authorship and provenance of the plate became the priority. Magnus contacted museums and specialists worldwide. Some replies were enthusiastic; others less so. Several warned of how difficult a mission he'd taken on. The first significant breakthrough came when the Picasso Museum at Antibes, in the south of France, referred him to the Picasso Administration in Paris. This establishment is run by the artist's son, Claude Picasso, who manages most things related to his father's unparalleled artistic legacy. Agreement from this organisation is crucial in sanctioning the authenticity of a work believed to be that of Pablo Picasso.

Magnus wrote to the Picasso Administration in Paris enclosing a set of detailed digital images of the plate. Their swift reply stated: "From the information provided, and only that, we do not think your plate is from the hands of Pablo Picasso". This rebuttal, although a set-back, didn't deter Magnus from his objective; after all the statement inferred that if some pertinent support information was provided the ruling may be reconsidered. As they hadn't examined the actual piece, how could they be so absolute in their determination? The course of action was clear; he'd take the plate to the Picasso Administration so they could see for themselves that they'd made a mistake.

Surprisingly, Magnus's research showed that the number of original Picasso ceramics remains in doubt; published estimates varied between 2,200 and 4,400 individual pieces. With uncertainty about the number of ceramic works produced, how can specialists be confident in their dictates on what the artist actually produced?

Magnus supposed that the more people who saw the plate the greater the prospect of it being recognised for what he believed it to be. In an effort to gain maximum exposure, he established an internet blog (picassoceramic.blogspot.com). The blog was readily achieved; the main problem was how to attract connoisseurs to the website. Googling Picasso produced 120,000,000 hits in 0.22 seconds, a formidable filtering undertaking for even the most enthusiastic art lover.

Whilst holidaying in London, Magnus arranged for several internationally renowned auction houses to view the piece. Unfortunately, his approach to Christie's was futile. As the plate had no official impressed stamping on the reverse side, they weren't interested. The cyphers incised into the back of the plate remained a mystery; perhaps they were the secret classification code which Picasso was known to have employed from time to time?

Bonham's response was very different from Christie's; they were keenly interested and photographed the plate for specialist review in an effort to establish authorship. During their research they forwarded digital images to the Picasso Administration who quickly replied: "We have already told Mr McAulay what our opinion of the plate is". This irrefutable reaffirmation of the Administration's opinion made redundant Magnus's proposed visit to Paris to take the plate for direct evaluation. The speed and nature of the reply demonstrated how complete, efficient and effective the Administration's record and retrieval system was.

When he contacted Sotheby's their response was instant and enthusiastic.

"Can you bring it over now?" was their approach.

"Good morning. I have an appointment with Jerry Noonan," Magnus advised the receptionist at Sotheby's imposing New Bond Street headquarters.

"An appointment with whom?" the front of house receptionist probed.

On repeating the statement, he was confronted with a blank stare.

"There's nobody here by that name," she stated, "…Jerry whom?"

He restated the name slowly and her face lit-up with instant recognition.

"Oh! Jerry. I'll let him know you're here," she said, with a hint of condescension playing about her face. "And your name again was?"

The whole exchange, even though masterfully executed, left Magnus slightly irritated as he believed she knew all along the person he wished to see. He well recognised a patronising put down when he was the victim of one. The receptionist appeared to be an employee making the most of her limited authority by giving the run-around to one ill at ease in unfamiliar surroundings.

She directed him towards the first floor where the meeting was to be held. Along the corridor, and at various strategic locations, dark-suited and wireless-wired security men stood fixing attentive eyes on all the comings and goings. Canvasses by recognised artists were stacked against walls in alcoves and hung all about in an oddly chaotic display.

Magnus stated his business to the first floor receptionist and a few moments later Jerry appeared.

"You can show me the plate over here," he offered, pointing to an area with a small table and two padded chairs.

"It reads like a Picasso. It's right in its vocabulary; more painting than ceramic," he stated enthusiastically, holding the plate securely in the crook of his arm, '....it's alive with his wit and playfulness. Where did you get it?"

Magnus told the story while Jerry painstakingly examined the plate and, after some time, stated with certainty, "No! It can't be a Picasso. It's too chromatic."

"You don't think it could be an anachronistic work?" Magnus pressed. "After all, his creative output from the potteries was anything but conventional, and its cataloguing, with the exception of the unique and editions works, is all but non-existent."

Jerry didn't think so, and advised showing the piece to as many specialists as possible. When Magnus offered to support his position with a photograph of another plate that was removed from Picasso's more usual ceramic works, and which was indisputably attributed to the artist, Jerry stood up to leave as though expecting a tiresome time-wasting debate. At that point they shook hands, and Magnus thanked Jerry for his time and advice. They parted amicably.

And so Magnus discovered there is little appetite for discussion or review when it comes to establishing the authorship of a work of art. The connoisseurs and doyens of the art establishment are indisputably final in their subjective and tribal judgements – rulings that may be tainted by the stain of scholastic elitism or the overweening pride of the aficionado.

These observations were dishearteningly confirmed by the BBC TV programme, *Fake or Fortune*. One of the episodes in the series investigated a signed Monet landscape painting which remained unattributed, having previously been rejected by the Monet Administration also located in Paris. After an exhaustive investigation by a team of independent and unbiased specialists and technical experts, the painting's attribution continued to be denied although all the Administration's initial concerns had been resolutely answered and assuredly repudiated. The reason given by the then Monet Administrator for continuing to deny attribution of the painting was that he couldn't go against the initial rejection of the work by the former Administrator, his deceased father.

This conduct suggests that even when confronted with positive forensic analysis, compelling provenance documentation and scientific evidence in support of authentication, the final decision may depend upon a subjective response based on a misguided sense of genealogical lock-step or latent antecedent intimidation. On the surface at least, this 'voice from the grave' ruling appeared to flout reason. Rather than engendering confidence in the official authentication process (which is presumably the purpose for the *Monet Authority of Last Resort* which rests with the current Administrator) it may achieve exactly the opposite effect, and in so doing, subvert the organisation's very *raison d'être*.

The inference Magnus drew from this and from his own experience was that those who had warned him of the difficulty in establishing the provenance and authorship of the plate had cruelly understated the obstacles to be overcome. Even so, undeterred, he forged ahead.

Having been suitably impressed by the diligence and rigour of the specialists engaged in the TV programme, *Fake or Fortune*, (even considering the Monet fiasco), Magnus applied to the BBC to have his plate selected as an artwork for evaluation in the follow-up series. Unfortunately, the plate wasn't suitable, the focus of the programme being on paintings and not ceramic works.

The avenues of enquiry were swiftly disappearing. During the following months he showed the plate to an academic specialising in Art History and Appreciation, who had written a book on the works of Picasso. Magnus was grateful to the Professor for making time in his busy schedule to offer an opinion but the meeting was to no avail; unfortunately, it was a typically hubristic performance by an academic confronting somebody he considered to be ignorant. That vacuous encounter left Magnus despondent; against his stalwart nature and better judgement, he was beginning to believe that the genesis of the plate would remain a mystery. That was, until …

"Am I speaking to Magnus McAulay?" the cultured woman's voice enquired over an echoing line.

"Yes," he replied. "What can I do for you?"

"My name is Dorothea MacCully, and while I am on the Island, I'd like to discuss the works of Willie Leece with you. Perhaps we could meet for coffee tomorrow?" she suggested. "Spill the Beans at ten?"

Dorothea was a strikingly elegant fifty-something, who flaunted her feminine jizz with the casual confidence of a much younger woman, its impact suggestively appealing.

"At the Kurt Schwitters exhibition last autumn, I was intrigued by the resourcefulness and novelty woven through the works of Willie Leece," she explained. "I tried to contact you through the Sayle Gallery, but you were abroad."

So there they were, six months later, unravelling the mystical praxis of the Manx farmer who had morphed into a sculptor of unique distinction. Magnus explained how the sculptural pieces were recognised as something more than just a reflection of the rural necessity to secure barbed wire, old fencing and bailing twine, to prevent them becoming entangled in cultivation machinery or ensnare the legs of livestock. Willie Leece used waste materials, and other farm scrap, with creative flair and humour to fashion distinctive works of art.

"Whilst pursuing the Willie Leece photographs online, I noticed your other blog: *Is this a Picasso?*" she said nonchalantly. "It's a magnificent plate. What's the story?"

Magnus explained how he'd come across the plate in France during a walking holiday and of his futile attempts to establish its provenance and authorship. Throughout the account Dorothea listened with a rare single-minded attention, akin to the legendary focus of Bill Clinton, a former American President.

When the account was finished, she explained that she was an art historian currently researching material for a book.

"I think we can be of great help to one another," she stated, smiling winningly. "I've dedicated my working life to studying Picasso, and for the past twenty years I've specialised in his ceramic works with a view to publishing a *catalogue raisonné* for this facet of his oeuvre. They're important works which have been too long misunderstood and neglected."

Now it was Magnus's turn to be surprised.

"I could have explained this straight away, but first needed to assess what manner of person I'm dealing with," she continued. "Amongst the dedicated and honourable that inhabit the fine art world, there is a cohort of charlatans and fraudsters who scavenge a good living hoodwinking the reckless and ill-informed."

"And how do I fair in your lexicon of personalities?" Magnus smirked with amused but lively interest.

"Let me put it this way," Dorothea replied. "The story of how you came to own the plate, although incredible, is entirely believable when you know the plate's history.

"You mean you know its provenance?" he probed enthusiastically.

"More or less," she replied, "although, until now, its current whereabouts remained a mystery. I even heard rumours that it had vanished into the Swiss black hole of artworks. There's a warehouse in the Geneva Free Port in which more than a million artworks, including around 1,000 works by Picasso, are secreted. They are stockpiled out of sight in wooden crates behind locked metal doors. Thank God that wasn't the fate of your piece. I've examined the blog images in great detail on high magnification, but need to see the actual plate to be sure. Also, several independent experts need to endorse my findings before I can go public."

"Why go public?" he queried. "You mean this work may be as important as I always suspected?"

"Let's not get ahead of ourselves," she cautioned. "If you're prepared to make the plate available, I'll arrange for my colleagues to examine it; then we'll know one way or another. In the meantime, I'll have them scrutinise the blog images."

The meeting took place a month later in London, at Dorothea's South Kensington home. Those present were recognised as Europe's most knowledgeable on Picasso ceramics. There was however, a single but crucial absentee; no representative from the Picasso Administration was present.

To intensify the near palpable sense of tension that pervaded the room, Magnus removed the plate from its cushion padding with slow deliberation. His reward for this theatrical ploy was an audible intake of breath from the illustrious gathering at their first glimpse of his find.

Each specialist was allotted exclusive access to examine the piece so they could independently document their observations and conclusions. After the inspections, all were supportive of Dorothea's assertion that there could be little doubt as to the authorship of the work. They gushed in admiration at Magnus's good fortune in finding the plate, especially in a rural French town famous only for large red chilli pepper, and doing so before breakfast as well. Mostly though, they pondered upon the improbable good fortune that led Dorothea, via Kurt Schwitters and the unlikely Manx sculptor, Willie Leece, to Magnus's blog and the link to Picasso.

"It's magnificent," Dorothea enthused after scrupulous examination of the artwork. "There can be little doubt it's the work I hoped it would be. It's even more wonderful than I'd imagined."

"Yes," Magnus pressed, "...but is it a Picasso?"

"No! It's not 'A' Picasso," she replied firmly. "I believe it to be 'THE' Picasso. Not just an original piece, but one produced by him with roguish intent."

During research for her definitive reference catalogue on the artist's ceramics, Dorothea identified several anomalous works he produced as demonstration pieces for other artists intent on following his lead into ceramic art. Dorothea believed she was examining the plate which Picasso made as a specimen piece for the renowned colourist, Marc Chagall, to learn from. At the time, Chagall had limited experience with the various decorative techniques that applied to ceramic art, particularly the use of chromatic oxides and glazes compatible with his colourful style.

In the late 1940's Chagall returned to France after wartime exile in the USA. He eventually settled in the South of France, close to the village of Vallauris. This community had been a pottery enclave since before Roman times and was where Picasso had almost singlehandedly revitalised the declining ceramic industry with his boundless energy and creative flair.

Always keen to be engaged with new and popular artistic outlets, Chagall also started experimenting with ceramics. This wasn't the first time he had followed in the footsteps of The Magician, Picasso. After arriving in Paris from his native Russia in 1910, Chagall sensed the new artistic fixation with cubism. He reworked and enlarged many of his earlier gloomy paintings in a fresher quasi-cubist style, an adaptation which quickly established his reputation within Parisian artistic circles.

Some overly critical pundits attest that Chagall fostered a career by painting variations on a limited repertoire of motifs, over and over, for fifty years. By contrast, Picasso lived in fear of inadvertently copying his own work. Robert Hughes, the renowned Australian writer and art critic for Time magazine, once wrote – perhaps unfairly – that some of Chagall's late works were 'cloying ethnic kitsch'. In the art world it seems Chagall remains a colourful, if contentious, celebrity.

"I understand Picasso's ceramics tutorial wasn't as innocent as may be imagined," Dorothea said to Magnus. She explained that during the early 1950's, both artists worked at the Madoura Pottery, where the doyen Picasso, who'd been immersed in ceramics for several years and had produced many hundreds of original pieces, was working close by the novice, Chagall. Picasso sensed Chagall was paying close attention to his practised handiwork, whilst feigning absorption in his own work. Chagall's temperament precluded asking advice from someone whose artistic equal he reputedly considered himself to be. He was an artist who, it has been whispered, amazed colleagues with his capacity to maintain robust hubristic stamina well into his dotage. Without a word being spoken, and in a mood of triumphalist wit, Picasso deviated from his typical spare style to produce a painterly and highly chromatic work which he knew the famous colourist, Chagall, was studying fixedly, albeit out of the corner of his eye.

"And this plate, Magnus, I believe to be the work produced that morning as a virtuoso's mocking piece, exquisitely executed, impishly dexterous, a *tour de force*; and now, thanks to you, gifted with an even more bizarre and treasured provenance than one could imagine." said Dorothea.

"Not only that," she continued, "but Picasso mockingly echoes Chagall's famous early painting, 'Self-Portrait with Seven Digits', by giving the knight on your plate one too many fingers on his left hand. It's fantastic, full of egotistical tension and the playful scorn of rivals."

"It would seem to be a significant piece of art history," Magnus mused happily. "But how do I gather sufficient documentary evidence to support your findings?"

"I already have access to detailed documentation regarding the plate's authorship and verifiable provenance up to 1998. Until now I had only a description of the piece, not a clear image.

To hold the actual plate is something I could never have believed possible. The thought of you carrying Picasso's most painterly ceramic work across the Basque Mountains in your backpack makes my blood run cold. This story has imbued the find and its provenance with a matchless romantic life all of its own. What do you intend to do with the plate?"

"Firstly, I must satisfy the Picasso Administration in Paris of the plate's authorship," he replied. "If Paris accept the evidence and attribute the work to Picasso, then it should be made available for all to see, not mounted on my wall at home."

"You don't intend to donate it to a museum do you?" Dorothea queried incredulously. "Have you any idea how valuable it is? At auction it may challenge even the choicest Hellenic examples or early Chinese Ming Dynasty porcelain to become one of the world's most precious ceramics."

Dorothea was a whiz with paperwork and officialdom. In only two months, all necessary documentation was compiled, indexed, verified, validated and dispatched to Paris for the Picasso Administrator's appraisal.

On the strength of Dorothea MacCully's name alone, most international art houses had accepted her endorsement of the plate and were vying to catalogue the work in forthcoming specialist auction sales. The plate's anachronistic placement in

Picasso's ceramic oeuvre, together with its aberrant provenance and bizarre significance in modern art history, let alone the uncanny allure of the piece itself, all combined to give the plate a matchless appeal to galleries, museums and private collectors.

Dorothea's connections paid huge dividends. Through interviews, newspaper articles, specialist journals, art publications and appearances on TV and radio, she'd generated enormous international interest in the piece. Expectations for the plate's sale were so high, and competition so keen, that one of the international auction houses uncharacteristically offered to forego its considerable seller's commission in order to secure the plate in-house for its publicity value alone. Estimates of the potentially realisable price for the piece were eye-watering, and if all went well, would leave Magnus more than comfortably off.

For all Dorothea's immersion in the promotion and authentication processes, she sought no reward other than to rest contented with her good fortune at bringing the important art work out of obscurity and into the public domain. There can be little doubt however; that the international exposure she gleaned from tracking down the plate greatly enhanced her celebrity as a ceramics expert and successful researcher. These triumphs lent considerable kudos to her enviable record of academic achievements and would undoubtedly promote sales of her soon to be published *Picasso's Original Ceramics: Catalogue Raisonné* and intensify interest in a mooted television documentary to follow.

****

All the while I observed and archived this unlikely cycle of events with amused, if incredulous, objectivity. I pondered upon the improbability that so unlikely a sequence of seemingly unrelated incidents could lead to the discovery and authentication of this earthenware masterpiece.

If, as many are inclined to believe, events are guided by a benign hidden hand which influences all, then for those who accept this creed, the discovery of the plate was nothing more than proof that such a power exists and the path of divine intervention had been followed with some, as yet to be determined, mystical intent; and all is well with the world.

For those who do not hold to this doctrine, unearthing the plate may be but another illustration that the whole of existence, including imagination, consciousness and ancestral memory, is the consequence of the unending series of random events that has been on-going, since time itself began, and possibly even before that.

Others, including my terrestrial host, Magnus, subscribe to Shakespeare's challenge to the limitations of human thought and language: 'There are more things in heaven and earth, Horatio, than are dreamt of in our philosophy.'

And as for what I later found out about these unknown unknowns, well ... let's wait and see.

****

Part III

****

THE FINAL ENGAGEMENT

****

Chapter 10 - The Berserker

****

This is the gateway to whatever was
And whatever can be.

The Time Lord (+2000 years old & still regenerating)

BBC Two: Dr Who, 15 March 2017

****

There was no sitting about waiting for the pubs to open in Magnus's retirement. His portfolio lifestyle was geared to be wide-ranging and engaged.

Even though his life was into its terminal quarter, and he was already halfway through that, he had everything to live for and knew it. Recent developments had spiced up his vitality with bonus zest that brought assured lightness of being, sparked a twinkle in his eye and rested a smile on his lips.

Life was good. He'd rarely known such contentment.

A publicity campaign would soon be underway to promote sales of his first book which he'd struggled over for several years. Umpteen versions of the manuscript later, it was suitable for publication by his cousin, David Seth, of Triskelion House.

Whilst writing the book, Magnus identified and celebrated a narcissistic nonconformity in his character. No matter how many times he revisited and corrected the manuscript, whenever he came across one of his own jokes, he always split his sides laughing.

All that is history, with the book made available through Amazon as both an e-book and a print to order paperback. It was finding readers, but few, hence the needed publicity and marketing drive.

A long-planned boat trip on the French canals was only weeks away, and if it proved to be sufficiently enticing, he would consider rearranging commitments so each northern hemisphere summer would be spent messing about on a boat along the waterways of Europe. The rest of the year would be dedicated to family and friends Down Under.

Magnus and his publisher cousin, David Seth, had planned a June trek along the 95-mile West Highland Way in the Scottish Highlands. This is the most popular walk in the British Isles with 65,000 hikers attempting sections of the trail each year, of which some 30,000 complete the distance.

September would see him once again team up with his Australian walking mate, Clive, to trek a different 250km section of the ancient pilgrimage trail, St Jacques, to Santiago de Compostela. This time the trail would lead from France over the Pyrenees into Spain and not along the coastal path they'd previously trekked. They planned to cover the distance in sixteen days, with a short stint of recuperation in Madrid.

And encouragingly, soothing noises were emanating from Paris about the authentication of the ceramic plate. Only minor supportive details had been requested which Dorothea considered to be more for form's sake than a serious challenge to the submitted attribution documentation.

All in all, 2017 was shaping up as a stellar year.

"I like the front cover of your book," the Sayle Gallery manager stated enthusiastically. "Is it from one of your paintings?"

"*Contemplation on a Broken Nose*," Magnus replied, handing over a dozen copies of the book for sale at the gallery. "It's from the painting on the back sleeve."

"Yes, I can see where the title of the painting came from," the manager laughed. "Rumour has it you're soon to return to Australia."

"I'll travel home later in the year," Magnus replied. "My youngest daughter, Fenella, thinks I've been living out of a suitcase too long. The death of my brother and several close Manx friends leaves a permanent void in life over here. My elder daughter and her family recently returned to Brisbane after six years living on Guernsey. The house I've been renting is to be sold, so it's time for a change. I'm ready to go home."

Gallery business concluded, Magnus headed for the harbour side marina to read the Saturday Daily Telegraph whilst sipping a bowl of café latte. He needed an interlude of calmness before facing the tedious aggravation of weekend supermarket shopping.

Saturday shoppers may arrive at the store in good humour, but few leave in such a sanguine frame of mind. Even in the car park, when confronted by a shopper pushing a trolley loaded with groceries, you'd better get out of the way, for they're coming through, no matter what. Weekend shopping relied upon pure necessity and a dogged single-mindedness. Once experienced, it's hard to imagine anybody shopping on Saturday afternoons for pleasure. Like dud lithium batteries, good manners are ditched in the supermarket's foyer.

As usual, the supermarket was choked with a crush of determined Saturday shoppers battling a congestion of containers, boxes and heaped vegetable cartons. The whole shebang was made worse by an endless stream of shelf-stackers' trolleys blocking access to goods and hampering progress along the narrow aisles.

Mean-mouthed shoppers extended as little courtesy to one another as bargain hunters at a department store New Year sale; it was every man for himself and to hell with the courteous notion of women and children first. Mayhem reigned everywhere; aisles were crammed full of gritty shoppers thrusting trolleys into every tight gap, clattering together, battling for space, no quarter given, none expected; and yet this was the Isle of Man, normally a haven of civility and leisurely service.

Warehousing goods amongst the shoppers may be viewed as a slick piece of lateral thinking by an ambitious store manager keen on boosting his own career prospects, but it certainly shortened tempers amongst their cantankerous customers.

Having been trapped amongst the heaving heap of humanity too long, Magnus scrambled for the exit as quickly as possible. Up ahead, a wide-hipped blond woman barged through the throng dragging a small yellow-haired girl towards the 12 items or less checkout. If he could have overtaken them to leave the warehouse sooner, he would have; but it was impossible due to an avalanche of advancing shoppers and the crammed aisle.

The blond dumped a heavily overloaded basket on the checkout counter.

'Should I point out that she has more than twelve items,' Magnus mused to himself. 'No! Leave it lie. It'd only promote aggravation, and she looks primed for action, no matter what.'

Ignoring the bustling madness all around, he waited patiently for the woman's groceries to be scanned and bagged. Moments later, the long nose of a high basket shopping trolley was thrust aggressively against his leg. Even amidst the squeeze of bodies, that was far too intrusive an action to be ignored. The trolley contained only a green, square-sided bottle of olive oil and a few packets of dried soup. Perhaps the jostling was an insistent hint from someone with few items to be allowed to check out before him. Sympathetic though he may be to any shopper's desire to escape the bedlam, there was no way he would move aside for any pushy sort. In that retail madhouse it's generally dog-eat-dog, with the possible exception of cripples or the elderly, who may exact civility.

Aggressive, pushy types usually provoke annoyance or challenge in Magnus. His instinctive reaction was to shove the trolley to one side, but he waited patiently, thinking, 'What the hell. Here, everybody's irritable.'

With a sharp and determined thrust, the trolley was again heaved forward. That was too much; something had to be done.

Reluctantly, but primed for trouble, he turned around to assess the developing situation, only to see a woman dash away leaving the trolley behind. In her eagerness to be free from the pressing throng she'd forgotten to collect some essential whilst cheekily reserving a place in the checkout queue with her shopping trolley resting against Magnus's leg.

He should have taken the opportunity to give himself space by moving the trolley away, but didn't bother, wishing to avoid unpleasantness and leave the madhouse.

Whilst the blond woman punched numbers into the keypad to pay for her groceries, the trolley was again jostled against his leg.

"And where do you think you're going?" he demanded of the thin-faced woman holding the trolley. "There's no room to move anywhere."

"I'm next," she spat. "I'm before you."

"Not a chance lady," he snapped back. "You're behind me and that's where you're damn well staying."

In simpler times, amongst lads at school, a dispute was resolved quickly with a punch in the mouth that may or may not have developed into a lively playground fight. Then there was no embarrassment; the issue was settled – not according to logic or justice – but with bare knuckles resulting in a bruise or two. The air was cleared, and other kids would be wary of the winner, and also the loser if he'd put on a good show. Battles, not brains, established the playground pecking order. At the age of 70, Magnus tried to side-step confrontation, wishing to conserve energy and peace of mind for more important things rather than squander them foolishly because of the behaviour of others.

'That's that,' he thought, a little shakily. 'Another pushy pest zapped.'

But no! That was only the beginning. Things then warmed up.

"She's before you," the blond at the checkout barked. "I saw her."

'How would you know? And what on earth's it got to do with you anyway, you nosey cow,' he thought, a hint self-consciously, as the ruckus was attracting mild attention from frazzled shoppers.

But instead, he said calmly, "If she was in front of me, then both you and your daughter must have walked straight through her, because I was right behind you all the way to the checkout."

He smiled warmly, while inside he was cringingly embarrassed, annoyed and acutely aware of the unpleasant spectacle in which he'd been cast as the unwitting delinquent.

"We're before you," the little yellow-haired girl whined, scowling up at Magnus accusingly.

"I know," he replied, fighting back the urge to say what he actually thought. "I'm right behind you."

"Now look what you've done," the blond woman spat. "You've even upset my five-year-old."

Even though he felt intimidated, humiliated and deeply isolated, he placed the shopping basket on the checkout counter with calm deliberation. The blond, her daughter, the stony-faced Asian checkout girl, and a score or so of frazzle-faced shoppers scowled in his direction. Throughout the unpleasant and undeserved exchange, he'd become the morning's entertainment; the scuffle in the playground. Like Hitler's denigration of the artist Kurt Schwitters, Magnus had also been unjustifiably branded as degenerate, an object of contempt, a loathsome queue jumper.

"You've only saved yourself ten seconds," his tormenter sneered, inflaming the already overwrought atmosphere, "…you stupid man!"

"After all the annoyance you've caused, you're not worth ten seconds of anybody's time!" he croaked, desperately trying to concoct something that would cut her to the quick.

"Oh!" she continued, scornfully getting the last word. "You don't want to talk things through then?"

Fighting back the frustration surging behind his eyes, he stood very close to the woman, and for the first time looked her straight in the face. Shockingly, she looked oddly familiar. As he glared into her bony face, it dawned on him where he'd seen her before. She was the oddity with whom he'd had a minor altercation the previous day whilst ambling along Strand Street, the town's main shopping mall. In the busy thoroughfare she'd galloped unseen alongside him, before unexpectedly cutting him off, with hardly a hair's breadth between them, as though he didn't even exist. Shocked at her audacity and rudeness, he deliberately didn't stop, but continued walking at his normal pace, which was perfectly measured to kick her ankle and stand hard on her heel. At that they both stopped dead in their tracks. She crouched forward and swung her head around towards him, her face contorted in mock pain and fury.

"I'm dreadfully sorry," he cooed, giving her a broad apologetic smile. "I didn't see you coming, you moved so fast."

The collision couldn't have hurt anything more than her pride. The shoes he was wearing weren't Willie Leece farmer-style hobnail boots, but made of soft canvas with flexible soles. With that, she lurched off feigning injury with an exaggerated limp and hissing through clenched teeth what he took to be a chilling Celtic curse. Seeing that, Magnus basked in the warm glow of the self-righteous, content with his quick thinking and spired reactions.

A day later, at the supermarket checkout, things were utterly different; it was he who stood in a mist of barely controlled outrage. He paid the bill with trembling hands, picked up the groceries and made to leave, only to be confronted by a young shaved-headed bruiser with the words, 'Be Still and Know that I am God', neatly inked into his scalp.

"You ought to apologise to that woman you pushed in front of," the self-appointed arbiter mumbled into Magnus's face.

Magnus's shoulders sagged, his head dropped and he sighed, "Struth! Not more."

Now he felt cornered, indignant and frightened of his own reactions. Argument was all but inevitable, and with that realisation all action in Magnus's psyche switched from 'Let me out of here', into a dull drone of slow-motion, even though reality was moving rapidly into no-man's-land.

****

Of course, I'd seen it all before. It's in the nature of the beast after all. He'd gone through life, not looking for trouble, but trouble seemed to seek him out, and I'd observed it all. Whether it was his manner, his stentorian voice, his penetrating blue eyes or just the fact that he had a mop of bright red hair that attracted attention, remained a mystery. The truth is, he'd frequently had difficulty avoiding the unwanted attention of others, and consequently was generally in a state of readiness if trouble came knocking.

***

"Pick on a pensioner is it?" Magnus spat back into the shaved-head's face as his strained emotional energy morphed into quivering, indignant aggression. "Mind your own business and piss off you holier-than-thou, tattooed turd."

Startled, the slap-top thug stepped back a pace, while his interfering dullard's brain unscrambled the exchange. Magnus had no idea if the bruiser understood the extent of his exasperation, but something registered, for the goon's face darkened, and in a flash he'd grabbed Magnus's front, shredding his favourite shirt and sending buttons flying in all directions.

"Don't talk to me like…" he hissed through thin white lips, but never finished the sentence.

Under threat, Magnus's insides coiled tight into a quivering knot of nervous fright, all will power burned, and with it his last vestige of self-control. In a red Berserker-like mist of readiness and half expecting an attack, he'd already dropped his shopping and was angled to retaliate. With all his force, Magnus slammed his forehead into the aggressor's nose which burst with a sickening, sharp, snap, jetting torrents of blood over his assailant's face and across his own chest. He should have answered his fear and made off then; but the seeing-red fury of the humiliated and unjustly served had taken over. In a flash he'd snatched-up a can of pitted prunes that had escaped from a fleeing shopper's bag and smashed it edge-on into the glistening red target that was the bloody pulverised nose.

****

Engrossed but detached, and powerless to intervene, I studied the battle as terrified shoppers legged-it in all directions. I (his perennial archivist) observed all with perfect clarity and recognised that he was out of control. Even though he's an old man, I'm acutely aware of the inferno his high-octane state may ignite and the price that might have to be paid as a consequence.

***

Groaning horribly in shocked surprise, his attacker slumped forward onto his knees. Magnus stepped back to finish the battle with a swift heel-kick, when, in a purple explosion of intensely bright flashes, his world stopped dead and he crashed full-length to the concrete floor, lying still, as though resting, as his father had done on Little Mill Road, Kerrowdhoo, on that chilly Saturday morning in March 1948.

In a state of vengeful euphoria, the hatchet-faced hag who'd initiated the conflict had seized her opportunity. She snatched the bottle from her shopping trolley, and with a wild, arching swipe caught Magnus a bone-crunching blow behind the left ear.

In history there is mention of noble beings, bathed with rare oils, participating in regal ceremonies. For instance, when Richard III, was crowned King of England in Westminster Abbey on the 6th July 1483, the new monarch was anointed with the purest refined sperm whale oil. However, there can be few in the history of mankind, who, when called to meet their maker, were crowned in a supermarket with a square green bottle, and anointed with a spillage of first cold pressed, extra virgin olive oil. For that was Magnus's fate; not written in the stars nor carved in granite, but set in the coagulating red blood that short-circuited his pulverised brain.

Part IV

****

A VIEW FROM THE ALWAYS NOW

****

Chapter 11 – The Novice

****

I see it is the whitest, frothiest, blossomest blossom
that there ever could be, and I can see it…
That newness of everything is absolutely wondrous…
The fact is, if you see the present tense, boy, do you see it!
And boy, can you celebrate it!

Dennis Potter (1935 – 1994)

Channel 4 interview with Melvyn Bragg, 5 April 1994

****

Magnus rests still but I'm no longer there. I've become part of the non-past – merged with the present tense. His body is on the bed, but I'm in every corner of the room, the volume of the room. As he wheezed his last breath, I'm released from my biological incubation to experience the first unfettered flush of liberty as the stillness of deep meditation.

The mood morphs from wondrous surprise to loss as someone enters the room.

"Oh Dad!" It's Willow our eldest daughter. She's stands still, just looking, sorrowful but serene. She takes Magnus's hand to comfort him, even though I, his essence, am separate from our still and silent shell.

There's blueness in the light now, a mesmeric blueness I'd known before, although this wash is weak and watery. The radiance fades to the greyness of a dull day, restful and soft, not uniform, but mottled and moving, lending no shape to the room or bed. There's a swirling haze, shot through by faded tints with no outline or boundary but alive with wispy activity. It's never still, but a soothing place where I slowly fade into a hazy vision of light, which now I'm part of. Yellowish edges drift like silken ribbons in a transparent sphere. Everything moves; nothing is still; all is formless, suspended in the profound peace that comes with silence.

Openings of pale hues appear then fade into the past, as though enabling access to a reclaimed Dreamtime. Colours wash through me, but I remain static, passing into the silence beyond. The only sense is an irresistible fascination in Being, no connection except through silence; there's nothing specific to engage with, except the ecstasy of awareness, as though immersed in a profound secret that's yet to be fathomed.

It must be later, for there's a group of people, a family gathering, with food and drink and lively chatter of happy times; no feeling of gloom, just celebration, reminiscing, enjoying shared memories. A stifled sob drifts forward to disperse into soundless warmth that fizzles to a forgiving softness.

Even though they are Magnus's (and my) nearest and dearest, there's a mystifying remoteness between those present and me, or at least that's how it feels in this airy state of unconditional love. Already I sense something other; it may be the unseen continuum of life's transcendental essence becoming manifest through me.

I feel 'thank you' to my mentor and host, which was Magnus's worldly being, that carried us through a lifetime of adventures and tutelage together. I've been his constant companion; the silent confidant within.

Thanks also to our two lovely daughters, our five grandchildren, and of course Sophia Elizabeth, the linchpin of our family, all of whom gave Magnus (and me) a joyous purpose in life. Oblivious to my presence, they relive old stories of Granddad's frequent rebellious adventures and mishaps, whilst I remain an intimate part of it all, the guardian of unblemished truth.

I drift with neither sense of time or being, nor anything in between, but alert as Magnus's memorial; the 'I' of eternal presence am free to flex and stretch from mere torpor into a niche within the continuum of terrestrial collective memory.

As though daydreaming through a wistful reflection on stillness and peace, a bewildering mirage materialises as the Isle of Man's Gaiety Theatre stage floating freely in a surround of impenetrable blackness. In supreme silence the curtains are drawn aside to expose an intense brilliance of mesmeric blueness that so beguiles the senses with its hypnotic wonder that I'm compelled to merge with its seductive embrace. But unable to move, I gaze in rapturous adoration into its infinite depth that so captivates every wisp of my ethereal self my only response is to surrender to its enchantment. All else is abandoned to an irresistible feeling of oneness and contentment. After a lifelong journey with Magnus Henry, to arrive back at the beginning and, knowing the place for the first time, to realise it's where I belong and yearn to be, ignites within me an overwhelming urge to remain.

Startlingly, a double act appears on the theatre stage. Dressed in black top hat and tails, sporting lacquered walking canes, glossy patent leather pumps complete with white spats, and with white carnations on their silken lapels, they tap-dance and twirl gracefully from the wings to centre stage. The look-alike phantoms of George W Bush, a two-term American President, and Tony Blair, a former Prime Minister of Great Britain, thrash, arch and gyrate in perfect unison through their slippery, well-rehearsed tap routine.

In a final frenzied outburst of clattering heel and toe tapping, the thrashing enchanters conclude the finale, allowing them to strike the classic Fred Astaire climactic pose, a stance designed to provoke the utmost audience adulation and applause. Standing in a haze of self-congratulation, bowing forward and down towards the stalls, lips wreathed with winning cap-toothed smiles, their left hands extend forward offering the upside-down top hats to the audience of one, whilst behind their backs, clutched firmly in their outstretched right hand, the silver-topped walking canes are held high in anticipation of a thunderous ovation.

In a silence that shrieked with the terrifying foreknowledge captured in Francis Bacon's portrait of the Screaming Pope, Innocent X, the black-clad cabaret stars putrefy and dissolve, layer by layer, from graceful ghouls, to mucous-like flesh, then crumbling bone. Ultimately, all that remained is a blood-red slime to leak through the boards into the dungeon-black orchestra pit below, there to disappear, for as yet neither has passed on, but remain unbelievably insistent in life.

Riveted in horror and disbelief, I watch a fresh mirage arise in the beguiling blueness, appearing as if immortal players in a phantom play. To my relief I recognise the troupe as old friends I've come to know through Magnus's interests and readings, living spirits, of indeterminate age, mustered from memetic memory.

Centre stage, Robert Hughes, clad in black-fringed motorcycle leathers, and Kurt Schwitters, resembling Rodin's cloak-wrapped Balzac sculpture, in a familiar floor-scraping overcoat and sockless sandal feet, laugh soundlessly at a smutty aside from a beaming, blue and white stripe-chested Pablo Picasso. Indistinct, towards the back of the stage, Willie Leece, dressed in his church-going Sunday best, is in cosy conversation with the svelte Winifred Prince, calmly fetching in suede-patched jodhpurs and loose, white blouse. Another trouper sashays from the shadowy wings to take the hand of the late Claudia the Sting, lounging seductively in a shimmering cat suit. He's well turned out in a sharp military uniform and at first glance could be taken for Charlie Chaplin play acting 'The Great Dictator'. Then I recognise him as the real thing, and, as though by osmosis, appreciate why he's here. Like it or not, in The Beyond, there are no refusals, judgement nor reward, and there is no retribution; just the unqualified testimony of each life's experience.

As one, the entire company of players stop their silent engagements to gaze directly at me, and grinning conspiratorially, wave welcome acknowledgement before slowly fading to disappear, leaving me alone with the purest cerulean blue of an infinite epiphany.

Sensing the rapture is about to be spirited away, I plead wordlessly, "Don't go! Please stay! Take me with you. Please! PLEASE ...!" But it's no good. The theatre curtains slowly close. The seductive brilliance of being fades to the black silence of oblivion. Only later, when the limitless void is too numbing to bear, am I aroused from the friendless torment of rejection by the single peal from a tubular glass bell whose lingering chime transports me back towards the forgotten eternity, hinted at in one of Magnus's poems: -

****

I Thought I Dreamt of Bells

No dream of common hue did charm so sweet a sound,
A crystal bellbird song that held the soul spellbound;
In soft sweet bliss my mind awoke amidst this mystic dream,
Of azalea mist in which to float in consciousness unseen;
So calm, so still I lay, lest one small breath did break the spell
Of that delicate bellbird charm, whose crystal chimes did love excel.

Warm perfume waves swiftly rose to drift and linger free,
As shooting stars reflected deep on a silver rolling sea.
What favoured me for such insight to breathe this mythic air?
So clear, so rich, this scented sound that did my soul ensnare.
In silken threads each thought was tied, except this sense of bliss,
A seductive smile of wafting chimes, a softened rainbow kiss.

No earthly cast did weave the web of this enchanted show,
An echo from a place, where home each soul must go;
Ribbons of light paint this picture serene in shimmering harmony,
To nourish the heart, to still the mind, to set the spirit free;
So warm, so soft, whilst bathed in light, although asleep, still hears,
That love, the key, the soul releases; the mists of life love clears.

****

... and I'm alone again, drifting aimlessly through an ethereal Never-Never, but now dreamily aware of being coaxed towards a perplexing premonition where time is meaningless, and into an exciting new phase of quantum existence that demands exploration.

With confinement over and gestation all but complete, my pairing with Magnus Henry's mortal existence is nearly ended. Once his physical body is no more, all ties unravel and I'll escape the quantum entanglement. In the meantime, I'll remain nearby to witness the dispersal of his body into its elemental, star-dust particles. Then finally released, I'll be free to follow the road not taken. And that'll make all the difference, again and again and again ...

****

EPILOG

****

****

In Memory of Cousin Ruth –

At the Gaiety Theatre

"The Diary of Anne Frank – Friday please."

"Stalls or circle?"

"What's available in the circle?"

"Front row."

"Circle's fine, although there's not much leg room at the front."

"A24's available and that has plenty of room."

"A24 it is then – Senior's concession?"

"That will be 10 pounds please. Would you like an envelope?"

"You recognize Alzheimer's then?"

"I'm just trying to please! Address or telephone number?"

"6620454"

"Donoghue?"

"No. Ruth was my cousin. She died two years ago."

"Shall I change the details?"

"No. Leave them as they are please. Peoples' lives are too soon forgotten."

"Here's your ticket. The theatre opens at 7 o'clock."

"Thank you."

Don't Forget the Mourned:

They Haven't Forgotten You!

****